Lost, Almost

a novel

LOST, ALMOST

Amy P. Knight

Engine Books
Indianapolis

Engine Books
PO Box 44167
Indianapolis, IN 46244
enginebooks.org

10 9 8 7 6 5 4 3 2 1

ISBN: 978-1-938126-83-3

Library of Congress Control Number: 2017957909

*"How art thou lost, how on a sudden lost,
Defac't, deflow'r'd, and now to Death devote?"*

—*John Milton*, Paradise Lost, Book IX

CONTENTS

Adam Brooks, 1945   9

Solution   13

Adam Brooks, 1948   21

Rescue   29

Adam Brooks, 1953   57

Retreat   61

Adam Brooks, 1957   87

Ceiling   91

Angeline Brooks, 1958   107

Velocity   111

Adam Brooks, 1961   129

Defense   137

Adam Brooks, 1995   159

Crawlspace   165

ADAM BROOKS, 1945

IT IS POURING RAIN. A good solid downpour means a day off from his summer job painting houses: sleeping in, lingering over breakfast, sharing a quiet morning with his mother, who knits and listens to the radio as he flips through magazines or works a bit at a translation, blowing pink eraser flakes onto the table, where they sometimes land in the butter dish.

He is considering his next move—it might be a good day for the library—when his mother grabs him firmly by the wrist. She is looking in the direction of the radio, the quiet murmuring of news.

"The President," she says. Adam wipes a crumb from the corner of his lip, irritated. He skims headlines but he doesn't like to follow the war news. None of it makes any sense to him. He picks up the last corner of toast and is about to pop it in his mouth, but his mother stops his hand in midair. "Turn it up," she says. Adam tilts his chair up onto two legs to reach the knob.

The bomb had more power than 20,000 tons of TNT, more than two thousand times the blast power of the British "grand slam," the largest bomb ever yet used in the history of warfare.

Now Adam is listening. He sets the toast back down. He knows what this is, even before the President can get the words out. He has never had this thought before, not in all his endless hours of study, but there could only be one way to get that much power into a single bomb.

It is an atomic bomb, a harnessing of the basic power of the universe. The force from which the sun draws its power has been loosed against those who brought war to the Far East.

The talking goes on for several more minutes, but already Adam is lost. Without realizing it, he has picked up a pencil and begun to sketch out an equation on the back of yesterday's evening paper, right under the weather report. He wants to run to his room, to start rooting through the stack of papers he's stolen, carefully, one at a time, slicing them from the bound volumes in the university library with a razor blade, to see if he can find the roots of this, begin to trace the thread. A lot of them are in German, especially the older ones, and Adam can't read the text, but he doesn't need to. The equations are the same. He knows there have to be more, many more of Einstein's papers that he has not yet managed to steal, perhaps even the ones he will need to really understand, but he has the nub of it. They are right there in the house, up one flight of stairs. His mother is holding his wrist again. She has more strength in her small hand than seems possible.

He cannot sit still. His body is made of molecules, which are made of atoms, which are bursting with the energy of twenty thousand tons of TNT. His brain is full of figures that can describe but never capture the immense power of the universe to create and to destroy, the rules that define its order, improbable but irrefutable. In the days that follow he will read news articles about three secret cities, in Washington, Tennessee, and New Mexico. He will see the photographs and learn the names of the physicists, some familiar, some not. But now, it is all he can do to keep his body from busting open.

The broadcast ends. He looks up to see that his mother is silently crying, her free hand shaking in the air.

The phone rings. A neighbor asks if they've heard the news, if they'll come over to drink champagne. The war is as good as over. Adam's mother declines, then phones her husband at the office. He is not in.

"Do you think there were people there?" she says, turning back to Adam, her lower lip trembling. "Where did they drop it? All those poor people. Their poor families." His mother had been a teenager in England during the last war, and Adam has been told the stories, but they do not come back to him now.

"Mama," he says, "They've done it. They've split the atom."

Years later, she would tell him that she had taken "atom" for his own name, Adam, that she thought he had been split in his mind, painfully divided in his heart between sharing her sorrow and joining the celebrations, and yes, these things are swirling around him, a nation split between victory and shame, caricatures of horn-blowing and hand-wringing, noise and high emotion and tears of every kind, but Adam is not a part of any of this. It riots around him as though he is a big steel bolt holding the spinning carousel to the earth.

SOLUTION

After dominating the southwest in the high school Math Team competition for three straight years, we had finally found the unsolvable math problem. At first, separately, we each thought it was a fluke. We were missing something. There was an obvious answer right in front of our noses, and we'd be laughed at by the others for missing it. But slowly, a whisper developed: I'm stuck. I thought I had it but it's a dead end. It's a trick question.

Not one of us could crack it. Not Joe Gemelli, whose father had been the head of the math department at Berkeley. Not Peter Gibbon, whose dad's job was so secret that even we, masters of gossip, had no idea which department he worked in. Not even Mrs. Feeny, our favorite math teacher, who volunteered her Tuesday and Thursday afternoons to coach our team. She'd pulled out the answer key after we initially hit the wall, and we heard her cursing under her breath as she worked. This was part of why we liked her. We also liked her because she managed to explain things to us without making us feel stupid, and because she drank Dr. Pepper out of the can when the rest of the teachers drank stale black coffee.

We slaved over the problem for all of the Thursday meeting, all of the Tuesday meeting, and all of the next Thursday, trying to get to the answer in the book. We worked alone, or in pairs, or, for a while, all as one. Once, Jennifer Goldfarb thought she had it, but she was off by two decimal places, and no matter how carefully we looked, we couldn't find where she'd gone wrong. Joe suggested that the answer key was wrong, but we rejected this idea—it was the easy way out. Laziness. Casting the blame for our difficulty elsewhere.

We didn't want to show it to our parents—we had our pride—but after four days, an unsolved math problem was more painful than asking for help, so we took copies home with us, stuffed into backpacks or folded into perfect, neat squares in our pockets. We didn't bring the loose-leaf notebooks we'd filled (we'd filled entire notebooks in those hours of trying), preferring to make it look casual. Some of us tried to pass it off as a challenge: we solved this. Can you? Jon Finke just left it lying around, knowing his father wouldn't be able to resist. Jennifer Goldfarb took her nearly-completed proof to her physicist-father and asked him point-blank to spot her error. Katie Brooks's mother, the chemist, took one look and pronounced it a job for her grandfather instead. "You can bring it on Sunday," she said. "Let him take a swing at it."

We found each other in school on Friday, and no one had yet cracked it, though our parents were busy at the lab, and to be fair, most of them probably hadn't given it much attention. But we were growing excited at the prospect of a new discovery. If none of us could solve it after days of trying, there had to be something there, some breakthrough to be made. "My dad took it to work with him," Peter Gibbon whispered into several people's ears during the day. We were supposed to understand this to mean that it was being taken very seriously. Perhaps the solution, when it finally arrived, would be the key to some invention that would save us all. Some of us believed it, and some of us just thought that Peter Gibbon was trying to get us to like him, because a lot of us felt sort of awkward around him. His clothes were very expensive, and his hair always looked wet, when the rest of us were lucky if our socks matched.

Saturday, we forgot about the math problem. We were just kids, after all, most of us between fourteen and seventeen. We had other plans: we rode bikes, or wrote poems, or hitched into Santa Fe to shop for tapes and T-shirts and candy. Joe Gemelli locked himself in his room with some magazines borrowed from his father's dresser drawer. Ryan Scarselli helped his mother bake and decorate a cake for his aunt's forty-seventh birthday.

There was one exception. Lorelai Halbroker had not put the problem aside. She'd worked on it Friday night until she couldn't keep her eyes open, then set her clock radio for 5:30 to get the maximum Saturday time in. When her mother rose at eight to make pancakes, she had already worked her way into three of the same dead ends we'd already explored. Poor Lorelai. She was always doing things like this, but it never got her anywhere the rest of us hadn't gotten already. Still, she was a nice girl. We liked to have her around. If we'd been honest with ourselves (though few of us were, at that age, or later), we might have said that she reminded us how exceptional we were, and that that felt good.

Katie Brooks spent Sunday working on her grandfather's old car, which he was teaching her to repair. It wasn't until Sunday evening, when the formal family dinner was almost at a close, that she remembered the folded piece of paper she'd meant to bring to him. She was nervous; though we would've all liked to believe that it was someone in our house who would crack it, Katie had the most legitimate claim. She had two parents and a grandfather who had serious, code-word jobs in the lab. Her family had lived here longer than any of the rest of ours.

After dinner, while Katie's little brother did the dishes, Katie ran for her backpack to retrieve the folded paper. She brought it to Adam, along with a cup of black coffee and a silver spoon, arranged on the saucer just the way he liked it. "I've got a math problem," she said.

"For school?" He took the coffee.

"Math Team," she said. "None of us can get it. Not even Mrs. Feeny. It's been a couple of days now." Oh, how we would've liked to be in that room when she told him that! We knew about Adam Brooks. Some of our parents had been fired by him, or at least severely reprimanded. We'd seen him around, with his wild white hair and his faded clothes. We'd seen his name in the local paper, or heard him snapping at the mailman or the janitor or anyone else who showed a hint of laziness. We wanted to get close, but we also wanted to stay out of the way.

"Give it here." He took the paper and slipped his reading glasses from his pocket onto his nose. Four minutes passed, and he neither moved nor spoke. The rest of our families, upon receiving such a challenge, immediately took pencils to it. They began sketching out possible solutions, choices for the route by which they might penetrate the puzzle. Mostly, they were retracing our own failed steps. But Adam just stared. Katie grew uncomfortable. Was he solving it in his mind, and any minute now, he would casually spit out the answer as though it were the easiest thing in the world? She hoped so, and hoped not at the same time. The rest of us, if we had been there, would have hoped only for the easy answer; by now we just wanted the problem solved, the solution explained, and if it was the genius of the town who explained it to us, all the better. But Katie, no matter how unlikely she knew it to be, wanted to work on it with him, making perhaps one small contribution to every four or five of his. She wanted the battle to play out in her presence, aloud. The silence grew. Perhaps he was growing frustrated. Perhaps our intractable problem had opened in him a pit of despair.

Finally, he spoke. "It's late and I've got data to review. Maybe another time." He pocketed the folded sheet of paper and went to his study. If we'd been there, we would've urged Katie to object. We would've demanded more information: Do you think you can do it? Do you have any ideas? Were we on the right track? But Katie had grown up around Adam Brooks. She knew not to push him.

That was it, we all agreed. It was time to give up. We had no more resources at our disposal. Word circulated through the hallways, into the different classrooms, some of us in English class, some in science and history and French, in different grades. Maybe there had been some mistake, a misprint, but we didn't think so. We'd been bested. We'd move on to other problems. We'd still win the state championship, and have a crack at nationals. For now, we had pop quizzes and research projects and college applications to worry about.

When we arrived in Mrs. Feeny's classroom for our Tuesday Math Team meeting, it was as though we had all witnessed some terrible act of violence, and didn't know how to talk to each other anymore as the people we had been. Joe Gemelli and Peter Gibbon seemed to have had some sort of fight, and were on opposite sides of the room, refusing to look at each other. Katie Brooks and Jennifer Goldfarb were side by side, reviewing their scores from previous exams, digging up the extremely rare problems they'd missed. Jon Finke had his dirty sneakers up on the desk and was reading a comic book. Ryan Scarselli was doing biology homework. Mrs. Feeny stayed at her desk, her head down, her face flushed. She was supposed to be our leader, and she had no answers for us. It was from her that we'd gotten the fateful problem to begin with. She'd even considered calling off the meeting that day; none of us felt like getting back to work on a new set of problems, even with the championship coming up next month. But home would be no better. How could it be that two short weeks ago, we had been an invincible problem-solving machine?

When he appeared in the doorway, our hearts sped up. Adam Brooks. Had he really come to sit beside us at our small wooden desks and explain away that complexity that had stumped us? It would be the career day we'd never had, because of course, we had no career day in Los Alamos. Nearly everybody's parents worked in the lab, in one capacity or another, and many were not at liberty to tell a classroom full of squirming kids what they did all day.

"Adam?" Katie said, part pride, part embarrassed whisper. She had never seen him during a weekday afternoon; he never left the lab until at least six, usually seven or eight, and she'd never known him to take so much as an hour off for a dentist's appointment. The dentist opened on Saturday if Adam Brooks needed an appointment.

"Katherine," he said, with a nod in the direction of his granddaughter. It was clear that he hadn't come to see her. "And you must be Mrs. Feeny."

"That's right, Dr. Brooks. It's an honor. Have you come

to—would you like—" We marveled at our beloved, tough-skinned teacher, stammering like a schoolgirl. But Adam Brooks ignored her. He went to the blackboard and began to write. After a few lines of forceful scribbling, his stick of yellow chalk snapped in half. Mrs. Feeny went scurrying over to him to provide a new one, but he waved her away, having already picked up where he left off with the bigger of the two pieces. We sat, our mouths open, watching. Before our eyes, he was solving our math problem. None of us had thought even of the first step he was taking.

"What's that you just did?" Lorelai said after Adam had begun a third column of silent writing. Our ears burned in the silence. We would not have dared to interrupt. We didn't know: was she oblivious to the power he wielded, or was she just that brave? Either way, we were glad she'd asked; he was moving fast, and none of us had followed it, not even Katie Brooks, his own flesh and blood. We told ourselves we'd remember to be nicer to Lorelai.

"Fatou's Lemma," Adam said, without turning around, without even stopping the frantic movement of his chalk. "Ask your teacher. I haven't the time."

"I'm sorry," Lorelai said. "It's just that there are some things in there that we haven't had before, and—"

"Be quiet, god damnit," Adam snapped. He filled up three and a half of the four panels of blackboard at the front of the room. Our mouths hung open. Our eyes were fixed on the stream of symbols. He circled the answer at the end—the one that had eluded us— with a screech.

"Voila," he said. "Knock 'em dead, kids." He turned to leave.

"Dr. Brooks," Mrs. Feeny said, "We can't thank you enough. Would you mind just walking us through your—" but Adam didn't stop to answer her question. He didn't even seem to hear her. He was already out the door, pulling it closed behind him.

We looked at Katie to help us interpret what had just happened—she could've been our new queen—but she looked even more baffled than the rest of us. She hadn't known it was coming.

"Would it have killed him to write it down and make copies?" Mrs. Feeny said, under her breath, to no one in particular. Our eyes drifted back to the door he had left through. It usually stayed open during meetings. We were wondering, vaguely, whether we could chase him down and learn something more. We were wondering if he would ever come back.

A sound came from inside the room. It was Lorelai. Her face was scrunched up so tightly we could barely see her eyes. She had been holding in her tears and finally she had let go and begun to cry.

"I'm sorry," she said. "I didn't mean to make him mad."

"Sweetheart, it wasn't you," Mrs. Feeny said. We considered this. If Lorelai hadn't voiced our confusion, maybe he would've stayed.

"It was," she said. "Nobody else interrupted him. I shouldn't even be here." Our faces burned. Our shoes pinched. Our palms sweated.

"Yes, you should," we told her. "If anyone should be here, it's you."

ADAM BROOKS, 1948

THERE IS AN ENVELOPE in Adam's mailbox. A business-size envelope of heavy cream paper bearing the Cal Tech crest. His name is written on the front.

It bears only a few scribbled lines:

Adam—
Please see me before you leave for the holiday. I have something to discuss with you.
Regards,
Carl Anderson

Adam exhales slowly. Professor Anderson is his assigned advisor in the physics department, and taught one of the two physics classes Adam took in his first term. He checks his watch, squinting and tipping its face in the darkness. The professor will already have gone home, and Adam will have to wait until tomorrow.

His mind is racing through possibilities, good and bad. He needs to focus all his attention on something else. The term has ended—there are no assignments—but he goes to the library just the same. He finds the shelf with spare copies of all the textbooks in current use; there they all are, without the usual gaps of borrowed copies. He pulls the text for the electrodynamics class he is hoping to take in the spring and starts with the table of contents. By the time the librarian comes into the reading room to shoo him out, he is well into Chapter Two, Electrostatics.

He sleeps poorly, and is out of bed early. He doesn't want breakfast, but he doesn't want to be lurking outside the door when Professor Anderson arrives. He gets himself two pieces of toast and a cup of coffee, though he has never drank coffee. He associates the smell with his mother, who had kissed him goodbye before school each morning with the smell of coffee on her breath, who writes him letters hoping to persuade him to transfer closer to home. He takes a small, tentative sip. It is hot and bitter, and part of him wants to spit it out, but the strong taste gives him something to focus on besides his own apprehension. He drinks the whole cup, one small sip after the other, then clears his dishes and walks to Professor Anderson's office. The door is open. He raps on the frame.

Anderson is a middle-aged man with heavy eyebrows and thinning hair. His office is cold, and Adam sees that the window is cracked open, letting in the chilled early morning air. He motions Adam in. "Now, Mr. Brooks, you're a bit younger than most of your classmates, correct?"

"Yes," Adam says. "I just turned seventeen last week."

"Well, happy belated birthday. Now, I ask because I'm sensing something in you that I see from time to time in students." Adam is barely breathing. His hopes are climbing. "You did quite well in your physics classes and I can see that you care very much about math and science."

"I do," Adam says. "Ever since I was a little kid."

"My concern is in how you feel about your other classes. Other areas of study in general."

Adam's heart pounds wildly now, that word, concern, ringing in his ears.

"Your scores were acceptable," Anderson says. "More than sufficient to pass. In both your German class and in Western Thought. But it's obvious to me, and to your other professors, that you considered them to be a waste of your time."

"Well," Adam says. "I came here to study physics."

"Yes," Anderson says, a terrible patience in his voice. "So did

I, a number of years ago, when I was a freshman just like you. But there is more to life, and more to being an educated man."

"I came here to study physics," Adam says again. "That's all I want to do. I don't want to be a philosopher, or a, a...a poet." He spits the word out with disgust. He thinks of the gangly boy in his high school class who was always getting into trouble with the principal for letting his hair grow too long, carrying a book around and bumping into things because he couldn't stop reading long enough to walk. He had come here to get away from such foolishness.

"I'll tell you what," Anderson says. "I'm just going to give you one assignment. You can do it over the vacation. And you must make a good-faith effort. Give it everything you've got, which I think everyone here agrees is quite a lot. You haven't any work in math or physics to do over the next month in any event, so it can't interfere. And then you can continue as you were, doing the bare minimum, if you still feel that that is what you really want, and you will get your degree in physics, and go off into the world and do as you wish. But I suspect you will enjoy it, and that it will be helpful to you, and I would like to continue these meetings and discuss things with you beyond science."

Adam sits in silence, betrayed. He'd thought he had finally reached a place where the most highly valued quality was one he possessed in spades, where extreme devotion to his precise area of interest was rewarded instead of ridiculed. And it had been; his scores were high, his classmates impressed. Boys in his house often knocked on his door to run things by him before handing them in or taking them up with a professor. Older boys had conversations he could follow, and into which he sometimes joined, to which he could actually contribute. And who was Professor Anderson to tell him that wasn't the way? He was no Einstein. No Oppenheimer.

"I don't think that will be necessary," Adam finally says. "If I did well in my major classes and passed the others, I'll just enroll in the next level next term."

"You need my signature," Anderson says. "On your enrollment form."

"I need instruction," Adam says. "In physics. In math." His voice rises. He feels the urge to stand. It doesn't matter that Anderson is his teacher, many years his senior. If the man is wrong, well then, he is wrong.

"Instruction you will get," Anderson says, mildly. "You needn't worry about that." He reaches to a shelf behind him and slips out a volume with a worn spine, its lettering too faded to read from across the desk. "I am only asking this of you because I believe you have great potential," he continues. "And I believe that this very brief detour may provide you with some context and methods of thinking that will prove valuable to you in your future work."

"What's the book?"

Anderson passes it across the desk.

Adam opens the cover to read the text printed on the title page. *The Collected Stories of Anton Chekhov, Volume II.*

"Your assignment is to read this volume and choose the story that is most applicable to your life. Whatever that means to you. Whether there's some moment or insight in one of them that feels familiar in your life, or just moves you for some reason, or if you detect some idea in Chekhov's thinking or observations, some quality in his values that you share. And then you must write a short essay explaining your choice. But in doing so, you must identify things you detect in the stories as a group, so you are able to explain why the one you choose stands out. If you just read one here and there, it will be apparent."

"And if I don't?"

"I suppose you were bound to ask that." This comment makes Adam even angrier. "It is possible that the chair might assign you a new advisor, though I suspect that most of my colleagues would honor my request that you complete this assignment before registration. Or you could come back and try again another term, when you are a little older. I suppose you could attempt to forge my signature. Or you could try someplace else. You really do seem quite brilliant, and I wouldn't be at all surprised if MIT would have you. But I do hope you'll just give this a try. There is room in your mind for more than you think. I suspect that this sort of exercise might even expand that room." Adam shakes his head and stands.

"All right, then," he says. He makes no attempt to conceal his hostility. "I'll just have to see about this." He is angry with himself for lacking a better response. He is angry with Anderson for saddling him with this requirement.

"Take the book," says Anderson. He leans back in his chair. Its hinges creak. "You don't have to decide this moment, though the harder you resist, the more I am convinced that this will be time well spent for you. Take it with you, and when you return, you can bring it back, read or unread, and if you don't return, you can send it, because it's a favorite of mine and I would hate to lose it."

Adam turns the book over in his hand and takes a deep breath. He feels the way he sometimes does when he awakes in the middle of a dream and can't remember what was real and what was invented. He needs to say something further, to bring this meeting to a close, but his mind is blank.

"Why Volume II?" he finally asks.

"Perhaps I will let you decide that," Anderson says. "When you are finished with this one, I will loan you Volume I to read all the rest, and tell me whether you agree that this was the better place to start."

"I never said I—"

"Oh, hush," Anderson interrupts. "Run along, you must have some beer to drink or whatever it is you do when classes are out. Come see me next month." Adam opens his mouth to speak again, to protest this infantalization, or at least to correct him and explain that he isn't about to go off drinking in the middle of the day, but Anderson appears to have engrossed himself in a pile of papers on his desk. Adam takes the book.

He doesn't tell anybody about his meeting with Anderson,

though there are any number of the guys in his house, all of them older and several further along in their studies, who would have listened and might have had some advice. For all he knows, he isn't the only freshman to have gotten this lecture. Maybe Fitzwilliam, on the second floor, got this same talking to two years ago. Or perhaps Pruitt, who is also from Iowa and has taken Adam to parties with him. But he doesn't want them to know.

As the day wears on and the conversation plays itself back over and over in his mind, he becomes more and more sure that he doesn't wish to return on these terms. Anyway, the faculty is diminished from what it was a few years earlier, and most of the men his high school physics teacher had mentioned as great teachers are no longer here. He could go back home and send in applications to other places. He could go to Cornell, or, as Anderson had suggested, MIT. He could go somewhere where he will be more appreciated.

The bus ride will take two days, and he's only been on the bus about three hours when boredom begins to nibble. He has flipped through the day's newspaper already, and everyone around him seems to be reading or sleeping. He tries to sleep and can't, the noise of the bus and the springs of the seat keeping him awake. He opens his satchel. There is a sandwich swiped from the house kitchen, his train ticket, the scarf he'd been wearing when he'd arrived on campus, which had remained balled up under his bed the entire four months he was there. And there is Anderson's book. He takes it out and turns it over and over in his hands. It has a musty smell, like the boxes of sweaters his mother hauls out of the attic every September.

He scans the table of contents. All the stories have names that seem incredibly silly to him, single words or short phrases, ordinary words that anyone could have written. He slams the book shut again, angry with Anderson all over again for insulting his intelligence. What sort of person would read a story titled "Sleepy," or "Boys," "Art" or "Love?" The stories, he realizes, must be quite short; the contents lists about a hundred titles, perhaps more, and the book isn't thick. Stories for children. Well isn't this grand, he thinks. Just grand.

He looks out the window but sees only dusty farmland speeding by. He doesn't want to read Professor Anderson's book, but he so hates to waste perfectly good time, and he hasn't brought anything else to read, having been required to return everything to the library at the end of the term, and having run out of pocket money nearly three weeks ago. He opens the cover again and slides his finger down the list of stories. He stops at random, turns to the appropriate page, and begins to read.

RESCUE

THE FIRST TIME I asked my grandfather for help, I was eleven.

I don't know why I did it. An impulse just came over me during recess, while the girls with their barrettes were off behind the swings in a huddle, leaving me to wander the yard on my own. He was standing alone, the skinniest boy in my class; a sunbeam was on him, and the wind was blowing hard, and I just thought, I bet I could do it. And then, I did. The stone arced perfectly, blown slightly off center by the steady wind, the force of gravity interacting with the upward and outward force I had applied exactly as I had known they would, making a perfect parabola, hitting right where I'd aimed, the spot at the base of his neck where it connected to his skull, where the curl of hair, that little rat tail, began.

At first he seemed all right. Surprised, he put his hand to the spot, then turned to see me. And then, he crumpled slowly, his ankles and knees collapsing as he fell to the blacktop in the middle of the four-square court that had been drawn there the day before with pink and yellow chalk.

It was this second hit—his head on the blacktop—that actually injured him. That's what they determined later, at the hospital, and eventually reported to me, after all the decisions had been made. The rock had barely left a bump, and no one was sure why it had even caused him to fall. But it had, and I had thrown it, and there was no getting around either of those facts.

If I had been a boy, they probably would have branded me a bully, a bad seed. I'd have been suspended, or perhaps even expelled, the boy's unexpected fragility my bad luck. But when the teachers came running and asked what had happened, and all the fingers pointed at me, I was met with puzzlement.

"Why did you do that, sweetheart?" they asked. "Did he do something to you? Was there something else you were aiming for? Didn't you see him?" I had no answer; I just shook my head.

"I don't know," I said, again and again, "I don't know, I don't know." I was sorry he was hurt. In that moment I had meant to hit him, I was sure of that, but I had not meant for it to hurt, and I certainly had not intended any sort of permanent damage. I saw it again and again in my mind, the knees, the ankles. I heard the thump. I closed my eyes and the playground was still there; I was still there.

They took me to the principal's office. One of the teachers had told him what happened, and what I had said about it so far (*I don't know, I don't know*), and he took me straight upstairs to the guidance counselor, Mrs. Hayes. He spoke to her in a whisper for a moment, then left us alone. He must have called my parents as soon as he got back downstairs, because I'd barely been there, failing to answer her questions, for fifteen minutes when they arrived together, in their work clothes, badges pinned to their pockets. They both looked at me, their mouths in little lines. I had thought my mother might come in beside me, lean down and give me a hug, or lay a hand on my shoulder, whisper something, *it's all right, love*, but she stayed beside my father, stiff as a stranger.

Mrs. Hayes's office had two rooms, a waiting room with a big square table where kids could sit in a group, and a smaller inner room with her desk and two big, soft armchairs. She'd been sitting with me in the outer room, periodically asking me questions as though phrasing things slightly differently might pierce the wall I had put up, then letting me be silent a while before asking another one. Did I dislike him? Had I wanted to hurt him? Did I understand that I had, in fact, hurt him? Did I understand that hurting people was wrong? Did I ever want to hurt myself? How did I feel now?

She led my parents to the inner room. She had a little machine that she switched on that blocked out some of the sound, but if I sat very very still and tried not to make any noise with my breathing, I could make out some of their words.

"A more thorough evaluation," Mrs. Hayes said. Then, a moment later, "The disciplinary process."

"She's never done anything like this," I heard my mother say. She was upset, her voice high and tight; it carried better than my father's or Mrs. Hayes's.

"Permanent record," said my father's voice. I thought about the boy, taken away in an ambulance. It had seemed to me that he was going to be all right; he'd sat up, before they led me away, and looked around. I tried to think about what it would mean if he was not okay, what would happen to him, and that it would be my fault, but I couldn't imagine it. Everyone had always been okay.

The three adults came out of the small office. "I thought we could all talk for a few minutes," said Mrs. Hayes. I said nothing. She tipped her head and looked at me. "Katie? Is that all right with you?" I didn't want to do it but it didn't seem that it was up to me, despite the fact that she was asking, so I nodded.

"And what about Mr. Franks? She asked. "Is it okay if he comes too?" I nodded again. Mrs. Hayes disappeared into the back room again to call the principal. My parents took the chairs on either side of me at the table. They were not full-sized chairs, and my parents looked funny sitting in them. I wanted to laugh at them, with their knees up high, but I knew that I should not, that it would make things worse for me. Finally, my mother softened a little; she reached out and ran her hand over my hair, then sighed. I wanted to tell them both that I hadn't meant it, that I was sorry. I wanted it to be just the three of us, like the meeting we'd had at home about the rules for the oven and the stove after I had set off the smoke alarms trying to make grilled cheese sandwiches for my brother and me one night when my parents had worked later than they'd planned, but they kept their eyes trained straight ahead, above me.

"Is there anything else you want to tell us about what you did?" Mrs. Hayes asked when everyone had taken a seat at the table.

"No," I said softly.

"We feel," said Mr. Franks, "that this would be better dealt with as a treatment issue, rather than a disciplinary matter. So if you'll agree—" he was talking to my parents now, not to me—"we can arrange for an evaluation and recommendation, and if you'll cooperate with the treatment plan, we will work with the doctor to get her back to class as soon as everyone agrees it is safe. We will consider it a medical absence." He turned to me. "That is, being out sick," he said. "No record, nothing in the file, just like if you'd had pneumonia. Can we all agree to that?" I tried to understand what he was saying, but he was talking so fast, and not to me.

"Am I going away?" I said quietly.

"I have in mind a doctor we know here in the district," Mrs. Hayes said. "And we will just see what he thinks."

My parents had not looked directly at me since they'd arrived, but now they both did. I could feel their questions: Had I really done it? Was there something I wasn't saying? Had I gone crazy? Was I really their daughter? *Yes*, I wanted to tell them, *it's me, it's me.*

"The alternative?" my father asked.

"It's an automatic one-week suspension for a first offense," Mr. Franks said. "It goes in any record we transmit, to the high school, to any other school you'd transfer to. And either way, we can't stop the boy's parents pursuing it. But that loses a lot of its force if you treat it this way." He took a breath. "In my opinion," he added.

My parents looked at each other. My father gave a tiny nod, and then my mother did too, as though by limiting the incline of their heads to just a few degrees they would make it invisible to me.

"All right, then," my mother said.

"All right, Katie?" said Mrs. Hayes.

"I'm not crazy," I said.

"We didn't say that, sweetheart," said Mrs. Hayes. "Don't worry. The doctor will just talk to you, and ask you some questions. He'll help you feel better. It will be just fine."

"We'll take you," said my mother. She touched my hair again, this time for a little longer. "You'll be all right," she said, though she did not sound convinced. All of this must have been far beyond their experience, any kind of misbehavior, any suggestion that something was wrong in the mind.

I expected them to punish me, but they did not. My father dropped my mother and me at the house, then went out to the store. He came back with a frozen pizza and two pints of ice cream. He was putting them away when the school bus stopped outside our house and my little brother climbed off.

"Why's Katie home?" he said when he came in.

"She came home sick today," my father said, and my brother accepted that without question.

My appointment with the school-sanctioned psychiatrist was at eleven the next morning. His office was two exits up the interstate, in a nondescript building that could have been anything. Only my mother went with me; my father went to work.

There is not a lot to say about the appointment itself. The psychiatrist was tall and thin and wore a green turtleneck sweater, and he made my mother wait in the waiting room even though she very much wanted to come in with me. He already knew what had happened, and he asked me a lot of questions, some of the same ones I'd been asked the day before but mostly new, different ones, which I tried to answer truthfully. I kept looking at the clock on the desk, thinking about school, about where I would have been at each of the moments. I would much rather have been in school; I had the distinct feeling that I was missing things that could be important, that even in the one afternoon and one morning I had missed so far, I was falling behind.

We talked for almost half an hour, and then the psychiatrist sent me out into the waiting room and my mother went in. Here, there was a thick, heavy door between the office and the waiting room, and the two couches were on the other side of the room, so I couldn't hear a thing.

"What did he say to you?" I asked when we left the office and stood blinking in the sunlight in the parking lot. There was a frozen yogurt store a few doors down and the smell of the cones baking was heavy in the air.

"Let's talk about it later," my mother said, "when your father is home."

"I'm not crazy," I said. "I want to go back to school."

"Nobody said you were crazy," my mother said. She unlocked the car and we got in and drove home. I couldn't tell if I was in trouble, or if they were genuinely worried, if they thought something was terribly wrong. Now I wonder if perhaps they were simply overwhelmed, paralyzed by the unfamiliarity of a contingency they had never accounted for in all their endless planning of our lives. My mother appeared neither angry nor worried. I wondered if the boy was all right. I hadn't heard any news but I didn't want to ask, thinking they would take it as a sign of something, that I cared too much, or didn't care enough. Everything I did or said had become a potential symptom.

I didn't have to wait long; my father was there when we pulled into the driveway. My parents went straight into their bedroom and closed the door. I stood in the kitchen. It was twelve thirty-five; lunch period would be over, and sixth period would have just started. English. We were reading stories that had come from The Odyssey, but it wasn't The Odyssey itself; we'd been assigned a thin book with an orange cover called The Children's Homer, which I found vaguely offensive. Still, I didn't want to fall behind. I had just started down the hall toward my bedroom to see what I had in the way of books— they hadn't given me a chance to collect my things, and had sent only what was already in my backpack, in the classroom where we'd left them before recess—when my parents emerged.

"Well, Katherine," said my father. "You understand, don't you, that we've got to cooperate with the treatment from the doctor you saw today? That it's the only way to avoid suspension from school and an entry on your permanent record?"

I nodded.

"The doctor told me," said my mother, "and I just told your father, that there's a place he'd like you to go, a different school from the one where you go now."

"For good?" I said.

"Not for good," she said. "Maybe just for the rest of the year."

"I'll get behind," I said. "I'll miss school."

"It's all right," my father said. "It's still school. It's just a different school."

"There will be other kids there who are confused about things," my mother said. "Kids who have had problems like the one you had yesterday. They know how to help." They were switching off, leaving no space between their comments into which I could have inserted an objection, a question, a sob.

"You might actually like it," my father said. "Some of the kids will be very smart, just like you."

"And then when that's done you'll come back to school here, just like before," my mother said, "and it will be like none of this ever happened." I might have asked them what the place was called, where it was, at least, but it seemed to me like something that was not actually going to happen. It wasn't real. None of this was real.

"We can talk about it more tonight," said my father.

"We've got to make some calls," my mother said. "And I have to go to the lab, at least for a little while."

"You can have lunch with your grandparents," my father said. "You can spend the afternoon there, and tomorrow morning, we can see what you'll need for the new school. They said you can start on Monday." I had never been to my grandfather's house by myself; we had always gone together, the whole family, or at the very least, my brother and me. I didn't know what I was going to do if he was angry, and I had no one.

In the car on the way to my grandparents' house, I wondered if anyone at school was going to miss me. There was Tillie Baker, who always sat next to me because our names were together in the alphabet. She would notice, at least, but I wouldn't have called her a friend. I don't know if I would have called anyone there a friend.

I realize now that what must have seemed like eagerness on my parents' part to get rid of me was probably something more like relief at the idea that this problem—of course it was a problem, their daughter having thrown a rock at another child's head—could be handed off to a set of professionals, who could provide a cure, with no permanent damage, and no need on their part to engage in an extended conversation about feelings. But it felt, at the time, like two of the only three people in the world (I would have counted my brother as the third) who actually cared about me were washing their hands of me, and it was this, more than the prospect of going away or falling behind, that pierced me.

My grandfather was not home when we arrived; he had gone to the lab for a meeting. My grandmother was sitting at the kitchen table with a stack of dog-eared books and a carafe of coffee. I had always liked her well enough. She was the only grandmother I'd ever had, my mother's parents both having died before I was born. I was barely in the door when my parents took off.

"Would you like to talk?" my grandmother asked me. I shook my head.

"About something else, I mean?"

"I'm already behind on homework," I said.

"Did your school send it over, then? Last night?"

"No," I said. "I just know where we were."

"I see," she said. "Here, sit. You don't drink coffee, do you?"

"Maybe," I said. "I've never had any." She stood—she was a tall woman—and retrieved a chipped white mug from a cupboard.

"I'll call them if you like," she said, pouring a steaming cup from her carafe. "I'll go over and collect whatever you're missing when your grandfather gets home. What do you say to that?"

"We'll probably start in a different place at the new school," I said.

"Well, in the mean time," she said. "Nothing like a little hard work to take your mind off your troubles." I thanked her and took a sip of the coffee. It tasted about how it smelled. The bitterness was unpleasant, but I liked it. "He won't be long," she said. My grandfather was mostly retired, though he still ended up at the lab several times a week, whether because they needed him or because he couldn't stay away, I never really knew.

"Okay," I said.

"Is there anything else you need for now?" I realized that I wasn't sure what, or how much, my parents had told them about what had happened, about what was planned.

"The boy," I said. "Is he okay?"

"I can try to find that out, too," she said, "when I get your school things. But from what I understand, he is going to be perfectly all right." I took another sip of coffee. I held it in my mouth for a minute before I swallowed. When I looked up again, my grandmother was reading, her elbow propped on the table, her forehead resting on her fist. I reached over and took the next book from her stack. It was a biography of General Eisenhower.

Adam, my grandfather, was severe, short on patience, and hated to be interrupted or to have plans disturbed. We always called him Adam—never "grandpa" or anything other than his actual name. He arrived twenty minutes later.

"Well, well," he said.

"I thought I'd go over to the school and get her books," my grandmother said. "A little old-fashioned work cure." Adam nodded. I imagined reaching out as she stood, grabbing her arm to keep her here to protect me, but she was gone. We were alone.

"I hear they're sending you to a hospital," Adam said.

"Is it a hospital?" I asked. "They said a school."

"It's a hospital," he said. "Whatever else they want to call it." I suppose I had known this, or at least suspected it, but the other words had lulled me. I had felt oddly foggy these last twenty-four hours and I was suddenly terrified that if I stayed home anymore, if I went to this school, this hospital, I was going to stay that way.

"Adam," I said, "I don't want to go."

"No," he said, "I suppose you don't." He paused. He pulled out a chair. "I understand there was a choice?" he said. "Hospital or suspension from school?" I nodded. "Your choice?" he asked.

"No," I said, my voice barely coming out. "I don't want to go. Please, Adam, can I just stay here?" The dullness of the last day was wearing off and panic was setting in.

"Tell me this," he said. His blue eyes were locked on me. He had fixed me in his stare before, but it had always been terrifying; now I felt I was the object of his true attention. "You threw a rock and it hit a boy on the playground in the back of the head. Is that right?" I nodded. "And it didn't seem, to anyone who was there, like it was an accident."

"Not really," I said.

"And the teachers and your parents and the school counselor and the so-called doctor have all said that you won't give any reason why you did that. You didn't hate him, he wasn't mean to you, you weren't afraid of him, nothing like that."

"No," I said.

"Well, Katherine," he said, "they're sending you away because they can't make any sense of this, and that's what they do with children who don't make any sense. They have no explanation, so they can't feel sure it won't happen again tomorrow, and if it did, they would be in a huge amount of trouble. They think there must be some kind of cause, because it's not just pure entropy that causes an otherwise kind and obviously intelligent fifth-grade girl to throw a rock at a classmate's head. If I were to formulate a hypothesis, Katherine, it would be that you had a reason, some kind of reason anyway, even if it wasn't a very good one, that you haven't told any of the people who've asked, and so that is what has gotten you on the next bus to Maclean."

"What's Maclean?" I asked.

"Never mind. If you've got even a shred of that reason hiding in that head of yours under all that long hair, and you want to turn this situation around, I'd suggest that you tell me what it is without delay, and we'll see if we can get this thing straightened out."

"I just thought," I said, "just right then when I was standing there and the sun was off to the side and I felt the rock and how heavy it was, I thought I could get the angle just right, the arc, with the force and the gravity, and there was this wind, and I—" I wanted to keep going, to finish my explanation, but tears had welled and my nose had stuffed up and I had run out of voice.

"Spit it out," he said.

"Just right when I threw it," I said, "I wasn't even thinking that it was a person standing there. I just calculated it, in my head, I mean, and as soon as I did I let go and, and, I just forgot."

"Bingo," he said. "I knew it."

"I didn't want to hurt anybody," I said. "Grandmother said she heard he's going to be all right, and I—"

"If you hadn't understood all the forces, you would have missed," he said. "It was a poor choice of target."

"I know," I said.

His mouth twitched. "Would it be accurate to say that you've just told me more than you've told anyone else about what happened yesterday?"

I nodded.

"They'll have to punish you," he said. "Testing a scientific theory on a classmate is a very poor idea indeed."

"I don't know why I did it," I said. "I wasn't thinking about that. I was just thinking about the wind, and gravity."

"That in itself can be the crime," Adam said. "But I suspect nobody will find that it is a mystery requiring hospitalization. Would you prefer a few days' suspension from school and a note in your record?"

"Yes," I said. "I just want to go back to school. And I want him to be okay."

"If it ends up on your record, it's something you'll be able to explain," he said. "I suspect some not insignificant group of the right people would find this story amusing, when you are a bit older and it is apparent that any shortcoming is only in a moment's overenthusiasm for the laws of motion. An important lesson learned, anyway, at a young age and without too much damage. There are plenty of men five and six times your age who still haven't learned it."

"I don't have to go?" I asked.

"I'll let your father know when they return for you this evening, and then we can call the school. Are we agreed?"

"Are they going to punish me?" I asked.

"I suspect that they are."

"I won't do it again," I said.

"You'd better not. Now grab me a piece of paper." He pulled a mechanical pencil from the pocket of his checkered shirt. "Show me how you did your calculation."

I hadn't wondered, at that age, how he was so certain that he could reverse the course I'd set off down, how he could undo the agreement, the recommendation, the referral that had been made, how he knew that my parents would agree, that Mr. Franks would accept the explanation, that no doctor would step in to say this child is obviously disturbed, and let's not be so hasty. But he arranged it all, and I was back in class two days later. He had made some small corrections to my calculation, and had drawn his own version of the path the rock had taken. I took the two small sheets from the kitchen notepad where these drawings were done and tucked them in my pocket. I put them in the bottom of my dresser drawer, where they would be safe, where I could look at them in the years to come whenever I needed to.

It was ten years before I needed him again. I had not seen much of him since I'd left for college, having decided not to make the trip back to New Mexico on any regular basis. I had gotten my degree and been accepted into a PhD program at MIT, had packed my things into boxes and been assigned an advisor: Dr. Lee Campanella. I had learned, via email, that my assigned office space would be in his lab, and I was to arrive for orientation on the fifth of August, where all the new graduate students in the department would gather before splintering off to our separate research areas.

My parents must have called Adam and told him I'd been accepted the moment they got off the phone with me, because the next day a bouquet of flowers had arrived at the front desk of my dorm. I'd called him to say thank you, but I hadn't thought to ask if he knew my new advisor.

Dr. Campanella's work was largely to do with neutrinos, which, with my thesis, was almost certainly why the department had placed me in his lab. I was eager for his return in three weeks from a trip to Italy, so that I could show him how much I already knew, and we could begin the process of figuring out what my own research would be, while I was here and going forward into my career. From the papers I'd read, I was optimistic that it would be an interesting and productive relationship, and I hated to feel the days ticking away. Two other students shared my office space and were assigned to his lab, Nathan and Samir. Both were eager too, though they had not read as much as I had, and were perhaps vaguer in their ideas of what they wanted from him when he arrived.

He came into our office on the expected day. It was two in the afternoon; Samir and I were working out problems from our introductory course.

"Hello, hello," he said. "Lee Campanella. Hopefully I won't be making any massive missteps to assume that you are Katherine and Samir." He was tall, perhaps six foot three, significantly older than he looked in any photograph I'd seen of him. He was bald on top but the hair he did have was long, gathered into a gray ponytail.

"Correct," Samir said. "Good to meet you." I wanted to tell him that I'd read most of what he'd published, that I'd been reading his work for years. I wanted to ask, or find some way to discern, whether he knew how closely my interests had tracked his. I didn't know if the assignments were made by some administrator, or if the faculty themselves looked at the files, the credentials, the applicants' undergraduate research. I wanted to know whether he knew of my grandfather. I wanted people to know about Adam, and didn't want them to at the same time. I wanted them to know where I'd come from, to understand that this was my world, not some choice I'd made by flipping a coin in my sophomore year of college. But at the same time, I didn't want to doubt that I had arrived on my own merits. My parents, of course, were not celebrities, but Adam was, or had been at least, in a way. I never knew if the name alone was enough; Brooks was not an uncommon name, and with the field ever-growing and the gap of two generations, it could well have been that no one would ever make the connection.

"I'll need to have all three of you in tomorrow. Class doesn't meet tomorrow, does it? Katherine, I'll have you first, at ten, and I'll see you, Samir, at one, and somebody please tell the other fellow, Nathan, isn't it, that he's at three. All right?"

We agreed, and he strode off. We could see him circling the lab from where we sat. It was a big cube, an open space in the middle with various desks and tables, offices all around the outside. He made his way to his own office in the back corner, where he closed the door.

"And so it begins," said Samir.

"Are you nervous?" I asked.

"No need," he said. "You're going first."

"So I am," I said.

That night I was excited as I lay in my narrow bed; my brain turned over and over the things I might say, how substantive a meeting this was to be. He had allowed two hours per student, which suggested that he wanted to discuss our work in detail. I had reviewed my thesis before bed, in case he had questions about it. By one-thirty in the morning, my mind was still churning over the consequences that could flow from this initial step, the path it might set me down that could dictate the rest of my life. I knew I needed to sleep if I was going to do well in the meeting, so I used a trick my father had taught me as a child for long nights lying awake, and began, in my head, to recite the laws of science, one for each letter of the alphabet. *Ampere's Law*, I said to myself. *The line integral of the magnetic flux around a closed curve is proportional to the algebraic sum of electric currents flowing through that closed curve. Boyle's Law. The product of the pressure and the volume of an ideal gas at constant temperature is a constant. Carnot's Theorem. No engine operating between two temperatures can be more efficient than a reversible engine.*

He was not there when I arrived in the lab. I had risen early and stopped at the bookstore on my way for a new notebook, half-page-sized and spiral bound with an orange cover. In my backpack were two blue, one black, and one red pen; my parents had taught me always to write in pen, the better to keep track of and learn from even the smallest mistakes. I waited in my office and, on the first page of the notebook, began a list of the things I might ask.

It was three minutes past ten when Lee Campanella stuck his head in and apologized for being late.

"No problem," I said.

"Should we go to my office or would you rather talk here?"

"Samir and Nathan may come in," I said.

"My place it is, then." His office was preternaturally tidy, his desktop clear, no piles of paper, no crumbs on the keyboard tray.

"Is it always this clean in here?" I asked. I was thinking of my father's home office, a tiny room upstairs that he would clean before he went on trips, staying up late into the night to deal with the contents of all the piles, leaving it spotless for his return, a condition that only ever lasted two or three days.

"I've got systems," he said. "Have a seat." The office smelled of lemon Pledge and tobacco. I looked down at the notebook in my lap, considering which question I might ask first.

"I know your grandfather," he said. "Or, at least, I assume he's your grandfather. In Los Alamos."

"That's him," I said. "He got me started. I've been working in a different area entirely, though." Lee Campanella swiveled his desk chair from side to side, then propped one loafered foot up on the desk.

"New shoes," he said. "Can't leave Italia without a pair. They just don't make them like this here. Of course, I had a look at your thesis. This is going to be grand." He asked about the thesis, about how I'd liked doing it, about what I might have added if I'd had the time and resources, and then we talked about the projects he had going and where I might help, during my first year, and then about what might come after that, research of my own, the particular questions I might begin to formulate, which of them were and weren't already being addressed, and at the end of the two hours, when I stood, half the new notebook was already filled with my neat black letters. He came around the desk and laid a big hand on my shoulder, leaned down, and before I even understood what was happening, landed a kiss on my right cheek, somewhat closer to my mouth than my ear, and whispered, "The future Dr. Brooks."

He was half Italian; I thought perhaps it was something he did with all women. The rest of the meeting had been so good, so normal, and until that moment I had been thoroughly excited about the work I would undertake over the next several years. I still was. But that night as I lay in bed, my mind wandered, not to the laws of science, but back to the kiss over and over—the closest thing to a real kiss anyone had ever given me—the smell of his skin, some kind of soap I had never smelled before, the weight of his hand on my shoulder. I imagined that hand sliding over my shoulder and into the middle of my back, and my whole body tingled the way I had always imagined it would, when, if, it ever happened in my life, that someone touched me that way. I knew I could not do it again, but that night I dreamed it, and the next night, too.

Thanksgiving: Lee Campanella hosted a potluck for lab members. He had been friendly but treated me no different than anyone else since our initial meeting. I had no way to cook in my dorm room so I brought a bottle of wine, advised by the clerk at the package goods store on what would be appropriate and cost about twenty dollars. I had not seen Lee Campanella drink wine, but I felt sure that he did, that he would have opinions, refined tastes. He came to the door and took the bottle from me, studied it and smiled, then leaned down and kissed me hello, casually, on the cheek, closer to the ear this time. My heart began to beat wildly and I told myself again and again that it was a holiday, a kiss hello surely bestowed on every woman who came through the door. There was a small crowd, Samir there already, and Barbara, a fourth-year student, and three other students from the lab, older than I was, whom I didn't know well, and several grauduate-student-aged people I didn't know at all. The air was already thick with the smell of butter and poultry and the sound of Charlie Parker.

"Bird," I said. "While you cook a bird."

"Clever girl," he said. "Your prize for being the first to spot my pun is a cocktail of your choice. I didn't know you were a jazz lover."

"The best late-night study music," I said. "Hard to get sleepy with all that energy." I followed him into the kitchen, where he immediately set to work mixing a drink, the choice apparently having been a figure of speech. What he produced was sweet and strong: apple cider, whiskey, lemon juice.

"I had a feeling," he said, "when we met, that you would be one of my Thanksgiving guests. New Mexico is a long way." I agreed. He excused himself to check on some dish or other and I joined Samir in the living room.

I had, by this time, told my parents, who had told my grandfather, who my advisor was. My parents, of course, hadn't recognized the name, but they had relayed from Adam not just recognition, but approval, a solid contributor with a clear head, a nice man, on the few occasions the two had met.

I drank my cocktail slowly, sitting on a leather sofa, and at some point the glass was taken from my hand and replaced with a full one.

"My family never did this," Samir said. "Even after we'd been in America fifteen years."

"Mine never really did it either," I said. "I guess it never really seemed important to them." I had never thought of it as a deprivation; I hadn't even really known or understood the holiday until I went to school, and then it became half a week at home, when I was free to read what I wanted.

Later, after maybe half the guests had gone, I was beginning to feel overwhelmed by the people, the chatter, the laughter. My quiet, small room in the half-deserted dorm called. I was in the hallway, the one that led to the bathroom and beyond that a staircase, looking at a collection of framed photographs on the wall. They were all black and white, and most of them looked old, people alone and in pairs who must have been members of Lee Campanella's family, parents and grandparents, aunts, perhaps, and even a dog, a German shepherd tall and noble on a rock.

"Lots of Campanellas," came his voice. I hadn't heard him approach, his steps muffled by the carpet. I had learned, without specifically setting out to inquire, that there was no Mrs. Campanella, that there had been one, briefly, years ago, but nobody knew much of anything about her.

"Who's this one?" He drew up beside me and followed my gaze; the man in the photo was young, and looked like him but with a longer face. He was leaning back in a lawn chair, outdoors, a cigarette in his mouth.

"My grandfather," he said "Guido. In Umbria." He was close enough that I could feel the warmth coming off him, feel him shift his weight from one foot to the other, and the first kiss replayed itself in my mind and sent its shivers through me, and before I could draw in a calming breath, he had turned me around, one hand on my back near my waist, the other on my shoulder just where it had been that first day in August, my back to the wall, him, kissing me, and there were no thoughts in my head, just the explosions of desire I had only ever felt in my sleep, as his slightly stubbled cheek slid over mine, as one hand slid up the back of my shirt. The part of me that knew this was wrong, that it could derail everything I had built for myself, was nowhere near loud enough to be heard over the roaring of need, of a voice that had been silenced for too many years.

And then she saw us: Barbara, on her way to the bathroom. Lee Campanella stepped away, and looked from Barbara to me. Barbara said nothing, just stepped past us and into the bathroom. He leaned in to kiss me again.

"No," I said, "wait."

"God," he said, "I've wanted to do that."

"She saw us," I said. I had known girls like this, girls who couldn't, or didn't want to, earn their good grades, who put themselves in situations like this as often as they could. I hated them, and Barbara, I was sure, did too, and I wanted to go chasing after her to tell her I was not one of them.

"Don't worry," he said. "Wait. Please don't think—I never do this. Not with a student. I never have. You're different, there's something different. It's you, it's how you approach things, it's something about you I can't resist." They were things no one had ever said to me before, and I knew it was wrong, but the words had a powerful effect on me. Barbara was still in the bathroom and no one could see us and it was a holiday and everyone had been drinking, and I leaned in and kissed him again, felt his lips part and parted mine.

The lock unlatched on the bathroom door, and I said, I've got to go, and retreated toward the kitchen looking for my coat, unable to remember where I'd left it, but of course it was back the way I'd come, in the guest bedroom down the hall where he was just standing, from which Barbara was now emerging. She fixed me with a look of such hatred that the currents of desire shooting through me turned to ice. I couldn't go without my coat; I had to walk five blocks, then take the T, and even if it weren't for the cold, the prospect of retrieving the coat at some future time from his house or even from his office was insurmountable. I had to get it now.

I couldn't see him from where I stood but I knew he was still in the hallway. More than ever before in my life, I wished for a friend, another girl who would be with me, who could see what I had gotten into and help me get out, who could go back there and get the coat for me, could listen to every detail and laugh at just the right moment. I had never had such a friend.

I went alone. I spoke when he was still four feet way. "I need my coat," I said. Then I added, "Dr. Campanella." He clutched his chest as though he'd been shot.

"Cruel formality," he said. "Come on. Just stay a while." He took a step closer and I pictured him sitting at the head of the long conference table where we had our lab meetings.

"I have to go," I said. Without another word, he stepped aside, allowing me to pass to the room where my coat, an army green field jacket, lay in the pile of coats I had seen come and go through the big double doors to our lab space, hanging on the backs of doors for the previous month or two.

I stayed away from the lab all weekend, something I never did but which seemed reasonable given the holiday. I reassured myself as much as I could that in all likelihood it would just fade away. There had been whiskey and wine and far too much food and an air of festivity, and I would forgive him his advance and he would forgive me mine, and things would return to the normal procedure, and Barbara and anyone else she might have told would see and understand that I worked just as hard as anyone else for whatever meager praise I could garner.

But that was not what happened. When I came into my office on Monday morning, steeled with resolve, there was a folded note on my keyboard. It said, "Katherine, Please see me. L.C." It was not scrawled on the back of some photocopied page of an article or a printout of some discarded data set as his notes usually were, but was on a heavy half-sheet of fancy ivory stock. I couldn't breathe. It could be a matter of punishment, of discipline, but I didn't think so. The severe tone of the note was not intended for me; it was for anyone else who might lift it surreptitiously from my desk, and for all I knew, someone already had. Maybe that was what he wanted, why he hadn't sealed it inside an envelope. I could've waited all day, and the next day too, but I knew I would have to go, and that the sooner I went the sooner I could get back to work, so I took a deep breath and walked around the corner to his office.

I knew before he said a word that all of my weekend words to myself, my reassurances, my plans to return to normal lab life as though none of this had happened, had been delusions. The voice I had silenced—the one predicting catastrophe—had had it right. He had never done anything like this before, he told me again, and he knew it was wrong, but he'd been fascinated by me from the moment he'd seen me, no, before that, and when I'd kissed him he knew, he just knew, this was it, it was love, and he wasn't married, and neither was I, and it had been sixteen years since his divorce, no, never mind, he said, don't think of it that way (I'd been five years old), and couldn't we find a way? We could, of course there would be some way, and before he'd said even half of these words I knew that even if it were all framed as a request, if he told me that it would be perfectly all right to say no, a return to my place as one of three first-year graduate students in Lee Campanella's lab was not an option.

Tears flooded my eyes and I blinked them away, because I had done it to myself, that moment when *I* had kissed *him*; I had turned my back on the dignity of my work, a steady and loyal companion for as long as I could remember, for the momentary flash of pleasure at somebody wanting to touch me. I had known it, had recognized the cliff I was stepping over, and I had done it anyway.

"Just think about it," he said as I edged out of his office.

Could I transfer to a different lab in the department? Everyone would know, and anyway, there was no one else on the faculty here who did the very particular thing I aspired to do. I could report him (to whom?) but I didn't see where that would get me, either; I'd be back to the same problem, if anyone even believed me. If I left here, tried again to begin the next year, this false start would be a stain on my CV that could not be explained away, if, indeed, I could find another program that wouldn't be put off by my present position. I couldn't sit in my office; I wasn't even sure I could *ever* go back to my office. I returned to my room and lay down on my bed. I pressed my thin, lumpy pillow over my face, trying my best to block out everything that had happened over the last five days. There was nowhere for me to go.

I lay like that all morning and into the afternoon. I couldn't, of course, tell my parents; even if I only told my father, he would tell my mother, and she would be so disappointed in me that I wasn't sure she would ever love me again, so intense were her feelings about Women Who Did What I'd Done. It was the very worst thing to be berated by someone whose criticisms are so piercingly accurate, whose utter correctness you already know far too well. I could've called my baby brother; he would understand the force of desire. He was a reader of poems, a brooder from behind a lock of hair he'd allowed to grow into his eyes, but the answer would be easy for him: if I thought there might be love, I should find out, and if I didn't think so, I should go find some somewhere else. There, again, was the hole where a friend should have been. And then, when I thought I might just die from anger and shame and loneliness, it came to me. I called Adam.

He listened, as I'd hoped he might, without interruption. "I know Campanella," he said when I'd finished. "But I've never known him to do anything like this." It was quiet for a moment. Then he said, "So you don't feel that you can stay, but you don't want to go."

"Go where?" I said. "There's no nowhere to go."

"We'll get to that," he said. "Jesus. Campanella. The man must be having some kind of breakdown or something. I mean, you're a lovely girl, but there are men in this world who do things like that, and Campanella, as far as I could tell, has never been one of them."

"Some of it was my fault," I said. "I kissed him back. Just that once, but—"

"I heard you the first time. You know, I'm not convinced you couldn't stay there if you wanted to. He's the one that will have to deal with it. These things happen. They've always happened. My first years here, everyone who wasn't married was sleeping with someone they worked with. And some of the married ones, too. And we all got our work done."

"He's my *teacher*," I said. "I would never know when he told me something about my work, why he was saying it. Why he was *thinking* it."

"You've made up your mind, then."

"Adam, am I being stupid? Am I overreacting?" I wanted to tell him that I couldn't assess this objectively, that I didn't know what I was doing because I had no way to know what a kiss or two was supposed to feel like, how two people usually met after such a thing and went on with their lives, or if they could. I wanted to tell him I was a stranger to all this, but as soon as I started to wonder, I thought of my grandmother, and of whether he had known women before her, and I knew it wasn't something I could say, not to him.

"I can't tell you that," he said. "And I can't imagine that a phone call form me would do anything to improve your situation."

"No," I said, "I suppose not."

"You could speak to him," Adam said. "Go into his office, and tell him that it was a mistake, and that you very much hope you can resume the professional working relationship you had."

"I don't know if I can," I said. I was crying and I couldn't stop. "I'm ashamed," I said. "And every day when I see him, I'll feel—" My voice broke and I couldn't form any more words.

"For heaven's sake," Adam said. "I can't help you with all that silly business. But I can probably get you out of there if that's what you want."

"It is," I said. I was certain it was the only way I'd ever manage to get on with work.

"I believe it may be possible," he said, "to get you a position at CERN, in Switzerland, for a year or two, and from there you could likely transition back into a very good graduate program." CERN was a large hadron collider, a state of the art research facility, where I had never applied to go, because they did not run a graduate program.

"How?" I said. "Doing what?"

"I know someone who has a team there," he said. "I suspect they could use you in a role with a mixture of technical assistance and theoretical discussion, for a year or perhaps eighteen months. A minimal stipend, I'm sure, but enough to get by."

"So I'd just drop out of MIT?"

"You could see about an administrative leave," he said, "if you think you may want to go back one day. I'm sure it could be arranged. You can always change your mind later if there's somewhere you'd rather go." He paused, then added, "Like Pasadena." Almost instantly, the crushing weight I'd felt began to lift.

"You must think I'm so stupid," I said. "I ruined everything in four months because, because—"

"Hush," he said. "I think nothing of the kind. Shall I start making calls?"

Surely I could have recovered from my twenty-one-year-old's certainty that the shame I felt would never fade. But what Adam offered was a solution to be implemented, one that put an ocean between me and the mistake I had made.

It was from the lab where I ultimately arrived, in Arizona, that I called on Adam a third time. A dozen years had passed; I was past thirty, and Adam was by all accounts an old man, no longer working regularly, though he still kept up with the field, and phoned me when articles appeared that he wanted to discuss. It was less, I knew, of a personal connection and more some mixture of relief and gratitude that out of a son, a daughter-in-law, and two grandchildren, one of us had emerged as a physicist, like him, a speaker of his dialect, a familiar soul in a room full of people who thought, by virtue of their similarities, that they understood, entirely ignorant of the differences and distinctions that made certain things utterly incomprehensible.

We had seen each other every year, sometimes more, since I'd returned to the southwest and was now within a day's drive; I often came home in December, when I had a break between semesters long enough for a visit but not long enough to get much of anything done alone in the lab.

I had been in Arizona six years, and would be up for tenure soon. There was another Assistant Professor in the department also up for review, and although on paper there was room for both of us, an independent up or down on each, it was reasonably plain to all involved that it was going to be one or the other. I knew there were those on my committee who would, consciously or not, rate me less favorably simply because I was a woman. I say that without self-pity, but as a measurable fact. I was angry about it but had come to the conclusion over the years of my uphill battle to get there at all that if I spoke out about it, I would become known as a feminist rather than a physicist, which would not accomplish a great deal for myself or for the women who came after me, my students and theirs, and that it was best to simply get as close as I could to the top.

The problem was that my competition and I were equally qualified. I needed to be indisputably *more* qualified, such that choosing him would be indefensible. I had a decent piece of research nearly completed, and I thought, if I could just place it somewhere truly great, it could make the difference. It was with this request that, on a warm Tuesday night in October, with two beers in me for courage, I called Adam.

"My dear," he said. "How are the mighty saguaros?" He had never traveled to Arizona but had taken an interest in the cactus that grew here; on his desk he had a photo where I stood in front of one, contorting my arms awkwardly to mirror it.

"Same as ever. Old. Tall."

"And the fraternity boys?"

"Drunk. Tall."

"You amaze me," he said. "I don't know how you manage all this teaching business."

"I don't mind it. I just wish it didn't take up so much time."

"Well, I suppose I should be grateful that someone with a brain is doing it. People like me don't make new physicists, and I'll die, and then what?"

"Fair enough," I said. I would have liked to stall a bit longer, but I thought I'd lose my courage, so I forged ahead. "Remember I mentioned a paper to you that I was nearly done with? On neutron oscillation?"

"Sure, I remember."

"I want you to help me place it."

"You won't need my help," he said. "It sounded like a good piece of research."

"I know I can place it somewhere," I said. "I want this to be big."

"Tenure-big," he said. "This isn't about the quality of the work, then? It's visibility you're after?" I nodded, then remembered that we were on the phone and he couldn't see me.

"Yes," I said, "that's what I mean." He knew my review was approaching, and about the competition.

"No," he said, "I won't do that."

"What?" I said. I thought there must be some trick to this, a next step, I won't do that, but I'll do you one better.

"I'm frankly disappointed that you've asked," he said.

"But I always thought—other times, when I needed help, you've always—"

"To help you secure the right kind of training," he said. "There was nothing I wanted more. But training is over, Katherine, and I cannot lend my name to manipulate the system of review that separates the very best work from the merely careful."

"I just need the smallest boost," I said. "This *is* good work. You said so yourself."

"It is not for me to say," he said. I could see his face in my mind, his cold blue eyes. I didn't want to think so, but I knew it was true. He had a way of doing that. I wondered where I might have ended up if I had never listened to a word the old man said.

ADAM BROOKS, 1953

THERE AREN'T MANY WOMEN here, but there don't have to be, because this one, the one who has just crossed the street fifteen feet in front of him, is something else. She has messy dark hair and green eyes, and she is tall—Adam would guess five-foot-ten—though she is often sitting when he catches sight of her. He has spied her in a number of places: at one of the long tables in the library, perched on a wall outside a classroom, reading a novel. Several times he has seen her in the dining hall with a man he doesn't recognize, probably someone in chemistry or biology. She is young, perhaps even younger than he is, and he avidly hopes that the man is a professor and not an overgrown graduate student, and that he is her father, or her uncle.

He also realizes that in a university of young men, he can't be the only one watching her. Others will know her father, will know what one ought to say to a pretty girl, and, for that matter, will care less about their coursework so as to give them time to go chasing after her. This is not a contest he can win with his academic clout. So he just watches her, whenever she appears, and secretly enjoys those moments. He takes pleasure in the slight tilt of her head, in the way strands escape from the knot at the back of her neck. Once, he'd lain awake at night unable to stop thinking about her, wondering what he might say if he approached, wondering what she might say if he approached, and he'd only been able to get his mind off her by getting out of bed and working a series of equations at his desk.

After a few weeks he has realized that it's on Wednesdays and sometimes Saturdays that she appears for dinner. The professor is Dick Travis, in chemistry; Adam saw his photo on a poster for a lecture. He has wished to keep this fascination to himself. It might damage his image, and he likes being seen as something apart, propelling himself past his classmates' levels of understanding without ever displaying the usual human needs. If anyone could read his thoughts now, he would seem just like one of those boys roaring away in a convertible on Friday nights and spending the weekend doing God knows what in Los Angeles.

It's 5:30 on a Wednesday and Chuck, his roommate, is putting on his shoes, ready to leave for dinner. Professor Travis and the girl come a bit later, 6, or even 6:30, and if they go now he may miss them entirely. Chuck looks over at him. "Well?" he says. "You coming, Junior?" A nickname they've given him mostly in jest; he is, in fact, the youngest graduate student in the department, but also indisputably among the most senior in terms of scientific understanding.

"I—I've got an equation to work out first," Adam says. "Just something I wanted to finish up."

"A likely story." Chuck is right; if there were anything urgent, Adam would've been doing it already, but instead he is stretched out on his thin mattress, his feet propped on a stack of blankets. "Who are you avoiding?"

"I'm just not hungry yet," Adam says.

"You are the worst liar I have ever met."

"Fine. Do you know Dick Travis?" he asks. "Chemistry?"

"I can't say that I do."

"Some days when he comes to dinner, he has this girl with him. I think it's his daughter."

"Oh, baby," Chuck says. Then, "you want me to sit here hungry for an hour so you can stare at a girl you're never going to talk to?"

"That's the long and short of it." Adam's face begins to burn, and he thinks he might just stay right here, in this cramped dorm room, for the next few weeks. He hates that Chuck has read him so easily, hates that he is right.

"Well, only one thing to do about that," Chuck says.

"Oh, no."

"Oh, yes. We'll go at five past six, and I'll bet she'll be there, I think I know the one you mean, and from the first sighting, you've got ten minutes before I go talk to her."

"No, no, no," Adam says. "Let's just forget it. We can eat in town, at the diner. Later. Let's go to the lab, what do you say?"

"You don't have to come," Chuck says. "That'll make it even easier on me when I sweep her off her feet. But if you do want to come, I'd wash up first. You've got pencil smudges all over you."

They leave the room at five to six. Chuck is kind enough to stay silent as they mount the steps, and even, miraculously, when they catch sight of her, toward the end of the buffet line, holding her plate without a tray, balancing a fork across it. She is wearing a dark green sweater.

"Clock's ticking," Chuck whispers in his ear. Adam looks wildly around the room. There has to be a way to talk to her without walking up to the table where she's sitting with her father.

"Can we set the deadline at anytime before she leaves?" Adam says. "I have a plan."

"If they head for the door I'm chasing them."

"Deal."

Adam hastily fills his plate with more food than he wants, soggy green beans, a rubbery pork chop, and takes a seat with his back to her. Chuck sits across from him, facing the girl. Adam keeps his eyes down as he mechanically cuts his meat and chews, spears one bland green bean after another. He senses that Chuck is watching him, trying his hardest not to laugh at Adam's discomfort. Two more guys join them, Ted from the lab across the hall and his roommate whose name Adam can never remember, and Adam barely says hello. Ted is trying to talk to him, to get his advice about a theory he's working out, but Adam barely hears. And then it is all happening at once: she is out of her seat, returning to the buffet exactly as he had imagined she might, having gone through the line the first time without room for dessert on her plate, and he springs from his chair to do the same, to the buffet table where she now stands over the plate of cookies, hunting for the one she wants, and then he is beside her, and he is telling her his name, his department, and she is telling him that her name is Angeline.

RETREAT

It was a cold day in November, by desert standards, with a dry wind and an early sunset, Halloween long gone but not yet Thanksgiving, when Celine walked out the door of my new house, and turning the powers of analysis of which I had always been so proud upon myself, I finally understood what the problem was: I was not a strong person. I could fight my whole life but I was never going to win.

It wasn't a question of desire; I wanted to stop her. I stood there forming the precise words I would say, shaping my mouth into the slight pucker needed for the "w" at the beginning of "wait," lifting the back of my tongue for "yes," but could not manage to generate the sounds. I wasn't even thinking of the consequences, what it would mean for my career, whether my family would be able to accept me if I put love so foolishly ahead of all else and threw away the work, the money they'd invested in bringing me back here, what it would do to poor Melanie, left behind here in a life we had only barely resumed together—I had already calculated that the prize was worth the price, that what I wanted was to go with Celine. But I could not speak. My father would always think I had made a terrible mistake, and knowing that, I could no more have chased after her than I could have lifted that house from its foundation with my own two hands.

He had sent a letter to our home in Somerville. It arrived on a Tuesday. Celine had set it on the little table that served as my desk, and though she said nothing, she kept peering over at me, looking up from the stack of papers she was grading, then looking over her shoulder while she stirred a pot of soup, waiting for me to tell her what it was. Later, I wondered if he had intended for her to see it first, if he somehow thought it was more likely to work that way, the wedge positioned between us before I had a chance to understand my choices.

He had found a place for me at the lab. *His* lab, in Los Alamos. The Human Genome Project was expanding, hiring microbiologists with experience in genetics. He had told some colleague on some committee that I was on the market, had provided a nutshell version of my CV, and on his recommendation, it was as good as mine. No teaching, no marketing, no FDA. I could start within three months.

Rather than explain all this, I handed his letter to Celine. She stood by the stove, her feet planted wide apart, holding it in both hands as she read. "Well I guess that's it, then," she said. "Should we say goodbye right now, or wait for three months?" I looked down at the letter in her hands, wondering if it said something I hadn't seen or understood.

"I didn't say I was taking it."

"No?" she said. "You're not? Your father summons you home and you're not going?"

"I have no idea. I haven't even had a minute to think this over. I don't know what else is out there. I—"

"It's a desert town with no university," she said.

"I don't need a university."

"Not for you," she said. She let the letter fall from her hand and it fell hard, without fluttering, to the linoleum. I felt like my throat was closing up, the thick smell of her broccoli soup making me queasy. We had not discussed our next move, studiously avoiding the subject, our love too young to face the test of that question.

"Don't be angry," I said. "I haven't done anything yet."

"You thought we'd just go our separate ways? A little company while you do your fellowship and then off you go?"

"Of course not. I thought we'd have another six months before we had to sort this out. That's more than a third of the time we've been together, and at the rate our relationship has changed in that time—"

"Jesus Christ. This isn't calculus." She pulled the cork out of last night's wine bottle and took a good slug.

"Easy," I said. "I just need to think." I tried to imagine it, and at the same time to imagine turning it down, traveling back for a visit some years hence having declined the offer, having, perhaps, some position that, whether I was happy in it or not, was less prestigious. I imagined traveling home from Madison, or Irvine, or wherever we landed, for Thanksgiving dinner with the McElhaneys, my parents' oldest friends in Los Alamos. *Isn't it a pity*, they would murmur to each other when I got up to use the bathroom, and what a silence there would be when I returned.

"I'm not holding my breath," Celine said.

"Give me a little credit," I said. "I can make my own choices." I believed it then; truly I did. I thought the strength was in me, that after all those months with Celine, with 2,200 miles between my father and me, that I was my own man. The choice, when I made it, would be the rational one, a job to be envied, a chance to contribute mightily to the field, and in a place to which I was not a stranger. It was my choice, and a good one.

"I give you a lot of credit for a lot of things," she said. "But Curt, I'm not blind. I've never seen you say no to him."

"You have, too!" I was furious with her for saying that. I had worked hard, the previous year, at her urging, to be independent.

"You're a smart man, Curt, but you've got a blind spot the size of Canada. You're going. I'll get over it."

"Are you trying to hurt me?" I asked.

"Just tell me I'm wrong," she said, "and I'll apologize all day and all night."

I'd only been back in Los Alamos four days when I saw Melanie. I wasn't sure it was her. Of course, I recognized her immediately—it's almost instinctual, with someone you've been that close to, even across decades, some kind of deep vibration not accessible to the mind, triggered, at first, by the smallest things, a car of the same model and color in some parking lot, someone in the news with the same initials, and then, as years go by, less, until nothing short of the woman herself would trigger it. I felt it when she appeared at the end of the aisle in the pharmacy where I'd come for a few basics I no longer wanted to borrow from my parents.

It hit first in my mouth, a numb vibration, as though all my teeth were about to fall out, and then in my toes and fingertips, dissipating and spreading as my mind caught up and I realized what I might be seeing. She hadn't seen me, and that gave me a minute to observe. Her hair was long, pale brown, uneven at the ends. She was the right height, about five foot seven. Her face was somewhat more angular, the bone structure more pronounced, but I knew it well. Yes, it was her, of course it was.

It had not occurred to me that she might be here, in all my endless mulling over whether I should come, and once I'd chosen, whether it was the right choice. That seems silly now; I don't know how I could not have thought of it.

Neither of us spoke for what seemed a long time, perhaps ten or fifteen seconds, until she rescued us from the growing silence.

"And I was so sure you'd never be back," she said.

"What are you doing here?" I asked. She was still perhaps eight feet away. I took three steps toward her.

"My dad died last year," she said. "My mom can't live on her own." There was no one else in the aisle, just the racks upon racks of toothpastes and mouthwashes, dental floss and denture cream, the vaguely blue fluorescent light. "Are you visiting? Is everything okay?"

"Everything's great. I came to work at the lab. The genome project."

"You're staying? You live here now?"

"I just got here. I haven't even found a house yet."

"I've only been here six months," she said. "Come on, let's go somewhere. Do you have time? Are you rushing off somewhere?"

"I don't start work until Wednesday," I said. "I've got time."

We paid for our purchases and I followed her to a coffee house that hadn't existed the last time I'd been home. In the car my mind was blank, the physical shock of seeing her there mostly worn off; I couldn't have said whether this was going to matter or not. A lot of time had passed since Mel and I had been together, years that really matter in the course of one's life, and I had never expected I'd see her again; I had neither longed for nor dreaded it.

The basic details were these: she, too, had found a job at the lab, though for her the move had come first and the job second, not a perfect fit, her skills underutilized. She was not married, nor dating anyone. It seemed awkward to ask, though I couldn't say why, all these years having passed, so I was grateful when she volunteered the information. She was living in the house her parents had moved to after she left for college, on the other side of town from the street where we had both lived as kids, which explained how I had been in my childhood home for three days without seeing her.

When we had said goodbye all those years ago—a dozen years, I calculated—we had meant it. There were to be no late-night phone calls from a dorm room in Massachusetts to one in California, no tearful, awkward reunions on holidays, no dangerous, lingering hope. I had never once asked my mother, when we spoke on alternate Sundays, if she had seen her, or heard anything about how she was doing. I knew, vaguely, that she had gone on from Bryn Mawr to the University of Wisconsin, but that had happened seven years ago, and it was the last I'd known. I hadn't even known for sure that it was, as planned, chemistry that she had pursued.

We parted at the end of the first cup of coffee. I sensed in myself the ability to stay a long time. Her company was easy; I did not need to explain to her the way things had been, and the way they were. But there would be time; here we both were, with jobs that did not expire at the end of some set term.

Now my mind was not so much blank as paralyzed. My life had doubled back on itself; everything I had wanted at the age of seventeen was suddenly before me again. I replayed the encounter as I drove down familiar streets. Was it ordinary friendliness, or did she sense possibility? Perhaps sense was the wrong word; perhaps all she had to do was to see the concordance, to marvel at the perfection in the timing, our incredible luck.

"That was a long outing for a pretty limited haul," my mother said, eyeing my drugstore bag.

"I ran into someone," I said. "We had coffee."

"Did you, now." She was rummaging in the pantry, lining up a row of ingredients on the counter, a bag of pasta, two little packets of seasoning. She turned around and looked at me expectantly.

"Melanie," I said. "Melanie Driscoll."

"And how is she?"

"She looks good. She's working at the lab." I paused. "Did you know she was back?"

"I'd heard." She opened the refrigerator and leaned in, searching the back of a shelf. "I haven't laid eyes on her," she added, her voice muffled by milk cartons and wilted celery stalks. "That must have been a nice surprise."

"Sure," I said. I hadn't wanted to discuss it with her as a teenager, and I didn't want to now. I felt nervous, the way I'd felt when I mailed off all my college applications and was watching the mailbox every day. It was a private suffering; even as a child, I'd been unable to bear my mother's sympathy for my failures.

"Well, I think it's nice," she said. "I wouldn't want you to come all this way, with your father luring you away from the life you had, and end up on your own."

"Noted," I said.

Her brow furrowed; I'd upset her.

"I'd be happy to help with dinner," I said, invoking a foolproof strategy from my youth.

"Wouldn't you like to rest? You must be tired." And I was; we'd spent a long morning, she and I, looking at houses without seeing anything that felt appropriate.

My childhood room was about how I'd left it. My mother had bought a new set of sheets for my narrow bed. They were nice, and must have been expensive, pale blue and smooth. On the sturdy wooden desk there still sat a jar of the pencils I had used in school. In the closet were a few items of clothing I had abandoned, corduroy pants with worn knees, a wool scarf and a couple of sweaters I hadn't wanted in Pasadena, though if I'd remembered they were there, they might have served me well during my years in Cambridge. I hadn't been much for posters on the walls, but I'd lined up a number of record albums facing out along the top of the bookshelf: *Revolver*, and Crosby Stills and Nash. They were still there, along with the dusty turntable. It was Melanie who had given me that second one, and we had lain on this bed, listening for footsteps audible over the harmonies of "Helplessly Hoping," while we pressed our faces into each other's necks, her hand slipping, impossibly, up the back of my shirt. It was at her house, next door, that we had later discovered the rest. Her house was two stories, her mother frequently in bed with a migraine.

Celine was Dr. Celine Garçeau of the English Department at Harvard University, an elegant woman, thin but not frail, five foot eleven, with skin that stayed impossibly pale in the summer, bright blue eyes, and smooth dark hair, her father French and her mother from New York City. My advisor had introduced us, though I've forgotten now just how precisely they were connected—somebody's cousin knew somebody's father, something like that. That was nineteen months ago. Fourteen months ago, I had as good as moved from my studio apartment on Garfield Street into her university-subsidized rooms overlooking Mass Ave, and seven months later, we had rented a place of our own.

We were both on two-year fellowships. On our first date, so

paralyzed by her combination of poise and unfamiliarity, I had stumbled badly, leaving long awkward silences, stepping on her foot. I'd thought for sure all was lost.

But somehow, impossibly, eight days later, she called. She was sorry for the delay; she had been out of town for a conference. She had enjoyed the dinner we'd had, and she would like to get together again. In fact, she wondered if I might be willing—if it would be appropriate—to show her my lab. And so she arrived, in high-heeled boots with a silk scarf knotted at her throat and listened as I explained to her the concept of an oncogene, as I showed her the freezers and the incubators and the sequencer.

"It's fascinating," she said. "It's unsettling."

"Unsettling how?"

"Well, when you think about it, everything about us comes from these little, what do you call them?"

"Molecules," I said.

"Yes, molecules," she said. "That we get from our parents and can't do anything about, and you've got this little machine in here the size of a small refrigerator that can unravel them and read them."

"That's about the size of it, I suppose," I said. "If you zoom out to the macro level. But we don't know what most of them do. I don't spend much time on all of that. It's all about what we can learn about one particular individual gene that causes a lot of trouble." Celine took my hand. She was trembling slightly. I asked her if she was all right.

"Yes," she said. "It's just a lot to think about." I had never seen someone react this way to my work before, but she was right; in a way, it *was* unsettling. Everyone I'd discussed it with before Celine had been accustomed to these ways of thinking. Even my father, who continued to insist that biology was not a true, hard science, had understood the basic questions of my work for as long as I could remember. Celine had a bit of a wild look in her eye, the way I felt at a party full of strangers, overwhelmed, searching for an exit.

"I didn't mean to upset you," I said. "Let's take a walk. Let's get away from here." I took her to a bar across the square where we could sit in a cozy booth and drink beer; I went there occasionally with labmates, and only after she had settled into a rickety chair did I see how out of place she looked, with clothes that surely had to be dry-cleaned. I should have taken her to the cocktail bar inside a fancy hotel. But she didn't seem to care as she gamely tucked her long legs out of the way and set her expensive-looking handbag right on the dirty cement floor beside her.

"Really," she said, "when you come down to it, in the long range, one could say that your work is to find a cure for cancer. Isn't that what you mean by the, the—"

"Oncogene?" I said. "I don't know. I suppose. Yes. But it isn't really—"

"And here I am," she said, "sitting in a little office tapping on a typewriter, words about words. I write words about words and I talk about talking."

"And people listen," I said.

"And then," she said, "they drink wine, and they sleep with one another, and drink some more." I didn't know what to say.

"I'll get us some drinks," I offered.

"Yes," she said. "This particular sorrow really ought to be drowned." I realized my mistake and opened my mouth, sure that I needed to apologize but unsure how. "No," she said, "I'm teasing. Relax. I'll have whatever you're having."

A warmth grew in me as I stood at the bar. I had never thought of my work as heroic, and no one had ever told me that it was; it was simply what I had always done, what everyone around me did, the same way we ate breakfast or rode bicycles. We had not, at some tender age, locked ourselves in towers to consider how we might make ourselves maximally useful to the human race and emerged with a plan. If anything, my work was small, confined, more or less, to the topic of humanity or at best mammalian life, nothing beside the great laws that governed every action in the ever-expanding universe. I explained this when I returned with a pitcher of dark beer, but it only seemed to interest her more. Two beers in, I began to be unsure which was which, my longstanding romance with research or my unfamiliar attraction to her. They had started to blend, my work appearing as it did through her eyes, her, a collection of organs made of beautiful cells made of molecules that were doing their jobs in the most extraordinary way.

I sat with Melanie in a Mexican restaurant out near the high school. She was wearing jeans, and her hair was pulled back tightly from her clean-scrubbed face in a way that made her look young and old at the same time, young because she'd worn it that way as a girl, because women I'd never known as anything other than adults, like my mother, like Celine, wore makeup, wore earrings, old because the changes are so much more obvious when the context is constant. I felt that I could have touched her, that there was no particular boundary keeping me from cupping the back of her head in my hands.

We had a corner table. The wall behind me was turquoise, the one behind her bright pink. We hadn't eaten in restaurants together as kids. We hadn't done much of anything, outside of homework and endless hours together in one of our houses.

"Is it good to be back?" I asked.

"Mostly not." She laughed. "You get out of here for a couple of years and you realize that humans don't have to live in deserts. That there are real advantages to living in a city that wasn't created with the goal of total isolation. Can we have a margarita with lunch? I mean, can we do that?"

"Sure." I signaled to the waitress. I wondered if she would've ordered a margarita at some other kind of restaurant, if she had grown into the sort of person who has a signature drink, if it could be something so elaborate.

Melanie said, "Tell me how you got here."

"My father's been involved in the genome stuff, you know, off and on, since it came out of the energy work. He knew they were expanding the team, and said he thought they could use me. There was no turning that down. Remember how we used to pretend we worked there? When we were kids?"

"Well," she said, "we did it. We're in." She laughed. Her fingernails were bitten down, her cuticles raw. "When did all this happen?"

"About three months ago."

"I was already here," she said. "I'd already been here for months."

"You don't think he knew?

"I doubt it."

"No," I said, "you're right, of course not." My father would not have realized she was back; he wasn't a man who paid attention to people who were not directly in his path. We'd had new neighbors two doors down when I was in third grade and they had been there nearly half a year when the daughter rang our bell selling girl scout cookies. He opened the door and barked, "Who are you?" My mother, embarrassed, had bought a whole case of thin mints, though neither of my parents was much for sweets, and we'd had them in the pantry for months. No, I didn't suppose he would have known, although there was a part of me that could imagine him engineering this entire life for me, right down to the cast of characters, the way he had always imagined his son would live.

"Tell me about your work," I said to Melanie. "Were you doing a post-doc? What did they find for you here?"

"I'd done a year in a lab, in North Carolina," she said. "It wasn't very productive." Our drinks arrived; her eyes when straight into her glass, as if she'd been just waiting for something that could absorb the intensity of her gaze. "Coming here didn't really disrupt anything."

"Is your work now interesting, at least?"

"It's getting there," she said. "I can direct the course somewhat. I think, as I get more and more settled, it will be satisfying."

"That's good news for the field," I said. I meant it. She was fiercely intelligent; it was one of the first things I'd known about her, a quality without which I knew we never could have generated so much as a casual friendship.

"Maybe I was always going to land here," she said. "Any mental picture I ever made of the adult life of a researcher had to be based on this. Yours too, I suppose. Other labs I saw always felt like they somehow weren't real. Like they were imitating this one, and failing."

There was, as there had always been, a real kindness in her that was never calculated, something that had seemed unfamiliar and wonderful to me in my youth, having grown up with the parents I had, with many virtues, simple kindness not among them. That, and she knew my family, knew my work; I had never, with her, had to explain or defend myself.

"Anyway," Melanie said, "I'm here now. And I imagine I'll stay."

"Permanently?"

"Well I'm not going back to North Carolina." She laughed. "That was a disaster. This salsa is really spicy. I don't remember it being like this."

"I think it changed owners," I said. "The building's the same but the menu's all different."

"I was married," she said, suddenly, quickly, softly, as though it were something embarrassing that she felt she had to say to me, a piece of spinach caught in my teeth, an obvious mistake in a paper already circulated. I looked at her, not knowing what to say. Somehow I felt I would have known, even across years of silence. "It was already falling apart," she added. "Before my dad died."

"I'm sorry," I said. I wanted to ask, but wasn't sure I wanted to know. I felt something I couldn't name. It wasn't jealousy – it didn't burn through me, and I knew she wasn't mine to claim, and I'd been with Celine, not just with her but in love with her, Melanie a tiny figure on the distant horizon of my memory, and anyway, it was over, this marriage of hers, but still I felt, against all reason, that in some way, she *was* mine, that despite where we'd been since and what we'd done, that was not supposed to have happened.

"I just thought you should know that," she said. "I'm sorry. I don't know why I said that." I wondered if I should tell her about Celine, but I didn't want to. It didn't seem related to all this.

"Who was he?" I asked. She was quiet a minute. "You don't have to tell me," I said.

"Nobody. He was nobody." She put her hand out, palm up, on the table, and I took it. Her hand was small and cold and familiar, and I felt it relax when I took it in mine.

Celine had suggested that we find an apartment one morning in her kitchen, while she was making coffee, as I was rummaging in her pantry for a box of cereal. "Bit of a waste," she said, "paying rent on two places when you sleep here five nights out of the week."

"Sure, I'll think about it," I said. Her face fell; she obviously hadn't expected hesitation. But it felt, to me, like a big step, like it would make me into a different person.

"We can forget it," she said. She turned her back, filling the water reservoir on the coffee pot. "I thought—well. I didn't think it was going to matter much. But if it's a big deal, if it's going to—"

"Just give me a day or two," I said. "Can you do that?"

Later that afternoon, when she was teaching her seminar, I called my father from my own apartment and told him what Celine had proposed.

"Well," he said. "Well, well."

"She's right about the money," I told him.

"And what about the rest of it? Honey, come home for dinner, honey, stay just a little bit longer, that report you're writing can wait another hour or two."

"You live with Mom," I said. "You've lived with her almost your whole career."

"Your mother," he said, "is a scientist." I had no answer for that. Celine certainly did nothing intentionally to interfere with my work, but even as it was there had been mornings where I'd had difficulty getting to the lab at the hour I'd intended. She had no lab. She had an office, but she also had piles of books and papers all about the apartment, and there seemed to be no particular boundary between the two.

"Let me ask you this," my father said. "Twenty years from now, will you be happy with a wife and kids and no serious contributions to the field?"

"Of course not," I said. "But who says I can't have both?"

"Why did you phone me, son?" I drew a breath and began, in my mind, to formulate an answer. But he spoke again before I had managed to pull it together. "Exactly," he said. "You already know what you really want."

After her seminar we went for a twilight walk along the Charles. I explained to Celine what he had said.

"You asked your father?" she said. "Why on Earth would you do that?"

"Some of us talk to our families," I said. "Keep them involved in big decisions in our lives." It was unkind—I knew her family was not getting along—but my mood had gone off.

"Well, he's wrong," she said. "I won't do those things. I won't make you come home. I won't make you stay. I couldn't make you even if I wanted to, which I don't, because I want you to do your work."

"You won't *mean* to," I said.

"It won't be any different from how it is now."

"It will be different because I won't have anywhere to go if I need to."

"And in those cases we will have to work things out together, and that is a good thing."

"He's not wrong," I said. "He never is."

"Oh for the love of Christ." She threw up her hands. "He's just a man. He's never even met me. You promised he would."

"I'm not sure that he, that you—I mean, the department you work in—"

"Jesus," she said. "You need help, Curt. You need professional help." She stood to leave.

"I'm sorry," I said. "Don't go. Wait. Celine." Seeing her back to me, I felt a kind of panic, a desperation I had only ever felt in a lab, opening a drawer of Petri dishes to see that nothing had grown.

"Give me one reason," she said.

"I'll do it," I said. "Let's do it."

"Yeah?" she said, one eyebrow raised. "You mean it?"

"I mean it."

"Daddy be damned?"

"Damned," I said, and it was the most thrilling feeling, free fall, where no one had ever brought me before.

The house I bought, perhaps a ten-minute walk from the one where I'd grown up, was too large, really, for me to live in alone, and my mother, who had actually seen it herself first, must have known that when she put it on the list. It was 2,500 square feet; it had four bedrooms, though one of them, cramped with no closet, was really suited only for a study. And with my whole family right here in town—there was no one besides my parents and me—there was no conceivable use for a dedicated guest room. I suspect my mother had in mind my sharing it, and with whom, but we couldn't discuss that while I was living under her roof, sleeping in my narrow child's bed, where she'd sat when I was ill or devastated by a test score or some other childhood failing, and she had tried, never with much success, to rouse me from my despair.

My parents loaned me the down payment. "It's the way of things," my father had said. "You can't save on a stipend." His first house—theirs, of course, but really it was his—had been provided to him by the government, the purchase of the big one I'd always known possible only later, after several years earning a decent salary and nowhere to spend it. Yes, they knew, they must have known, that they were buying something that would never be a bachelor pad. But if my mother had her hopes, had seen the reunion coming a mile away, my father wouldn't have realized.

I had thought of asking Melanie to come along when I took my second tour of the house, to sit by me while I signed the papers, but I sensed that it would look wrong from the outside, too hasty, even if we knew ourselves exactly where we were heading by then, if we could've gotten there instantly, having been there before, all the pieces lined up so neatly on the table, ready to snap into place.

I had no furniture—what little I'd owned in Boston I'd sold or left with Celine, who had probably put it out on the curb as soon as she'd left me off, kindly, at the airport. Melanie came to the house the second day after closing and we walked around in our socks. She sat beside me on the painted concrete floor and looked over my shoulder as I paged through a catalog to order some furniture, a king-sized bed, a dining set, a pair of sofas and side tables. Lamps and rugs, dishes, pots and pans.

"It won't fit," she said of a sofa I'd marked. "I mean, it will fit, physically, but it will overpower the room."

"Which do you think, then?" I asked, and she flipped a few pages ahead to a smaller, simpler one.

"You'll like this. It will work well for you." I froze. *I* would like it, she said. Me. Not us. She knew, didn't she? She must have known, with the big house, with the way things were, that it was for us. It was just part of the appearance, the caution we were affecting, the gentle brakes being applied, without changing direction, without any intention of coming to a stop.

I thought back over the last weeks, searching for a moment, any moment that, when examined closely, lacked ambiguity. We'd gone on hikes. We'd sat across from one another in restaurants. We held hands. Our knees could touch under the table and I'd remember some long-ago afternoon. Sometimes when we parted we kissed, gently, with dry lips. And then I went back to my parents' house and she to hers, and I imagined our life, our fingers intertwined, our work a success. There were phone calls. We had talked about our days, our plans. I was sick with it all, the thought that I could have misread it so badly, the thought that she wouldn't want this, that I would be here, in this big house, alone.

The days that followed did nothing to allay my fears. She was harder to get ahold of. I felt, listening to the phone ring endlessly, that she was avoiding me, and when we did meet, she didn't meet my eyes. "Goodnight," she'd say, jumping out of the car and slamming the door without looking back. Had she sensed my misunderstanding, and engaged in a campaign to make herself clear? Had I said something to upset her? It didn't seem possible, but could it be that she hadn't changed at all, and I had removed the filter of wishful thinking that had taken over all of my senses? I lay awake nights. I focused on my work as best I could.

Ten miserable days later, the house was finally ready; my mother had come over during the day to receive the last furniture delivery. Mel and I hadn't seen each other that day, her building on the other side of the campus from mine. After work, I drove to the supermarket, then home, where I let myself in without ceremony. I fried myself two eggs for dinner, thinking how stupid I'd been to buy a big house like this, to order a king-sized bed, to believe, with no real evidence, that she would come.

It was getting late, nearly ten. I was sitting on the small sofa, all the lights off in the house except for a reading lamp beside me. I'd changed into shorts, and had one bare foot up on the cushion beside me, a green cardboard folder in my lap; the adjustment period to the new lab, its policies, its people, its tasks, was finally subsiding and I had real work to do. It reminded me of my childhood; I had seen my father slide just such a folder from a briefcase. (I had no briefcase; I set the folder loose beside me on the seat of my car, and carried it under my arm). I'd brought a quart of orange juice over and was swigging from the carton.

The headlights swept briefly through my front window. I

thought it was a car passing on the street; I was immersed in my report, and didn't think much about the world off those pages. But as I reached the end of a section several minutes later, it occurred to me that my big front window, through which those lights had shone, was parallel to the road; the lights had come straight in, not oblique beams striking the wall behind me. If I had been there more than a week, of course I would have known this. It would have been obvious and familiar: there was a car in my driveway. It had pulled in and switched off its lights.

I set down the folder and went to the window. In the faint faded glow of the day, still lingering at that hour, desert in June, I could see her light blue Honda sitting there. She was in the driver's seat, her hands in her lap. She sat completely still.

I went out through the front door, leaving it open behind me. She looked up at the noise, and turned her face away a moment. Then she cranked the window down a few inches. "I wasn't sure you were home," she said. "The house is dark."

"Come in," I said. "I can make tea. Do you want tea? I don't think I have any wine, or—"

"You were going to bed," she said. "I never should have come. It's just, I went back to the lab, I was sure I'd left something on, and then I was driving by."

"Come in," I said again. I stepped back from the car so she could open the door. I tried to open it myself, but it was locked. I vividly remembered bringing her inside in a hurry, desperate not to waste any precious minutes, the evening in our junior year when my parents had gone out to dinner in Santa Fe for their anniversary. She was watching for their car to turn right at the end of the road, to disappear; we'd agreed to wait four minutes.

She followed my eyes to the front door, standing open. "Just for a few minutes," she said. She got out of the car. There was a floral smell, perhaps her shampoo, an after-work shower.

I closed the door behind us and flicked on a light. The entranceway was bare; the simple list I'd drawn up had not included a coat rack or a little table to stand in the hall, collecting keys and mail, nor lamps or rugs enough to fill a space of this size, and it still had a temporary feeling, like a furnished apartment on the market.

"Do you want that tea?" She shook her head. She led me by the hand to the couch where I'd been reading, the one she'd picked out. I sat with my feet on the floor and she sat cross-legged, her left knee falling into my lap, just lightly enough that it might have been accidental; if we were seated that way in a crowded room, no one might have noticed anything at all between us. I looked up at the bare wall, then over at her. Without planning, without thought, I did the next thing, and the next: I leaned over and kissed her lightly, just beside her mouth. I wrapped my arms gently around her and allowed her to kiss me back, not so lightly, and I was flooded with relief: I had not imagined it after all.

After a minute she pulled away. "I didn't come here for this," she said. "I mean, I really did have to go by the lab, and I—"

"It's all right," I said. It was so quiet that I could hear water running in my next-door neighbor's pipes. We kissed some more, and she slipped a hand under the back of my shirt, and I worked my fingers through the hair at the back of her neck.

She pulled away. "I have to tell you something," she said.

"What is it?"

"I knew you were coming," she said.

"I don't understand," I said. "Coming where?"

"Here. Los Alamos. I was only going to stay here three months, and right as I was getting ready to find someplace for Mom to live, to get everything packed up, your mother came to my office."

My breath caught in my throat.

"She told me you'd taken a job here, that you'd be here soon, that you were coming back to build a life here. And she made me promise not to tell you."

It took me some time to absorb this, to understand what she was telling me. Our first meeting in the drug store, her carefully constructed words, questions to which she must have already known the answers.

"You stayed here because of me?"

"I know, it's pathetic, it's terrible, but I was just so lonely, and when we were kids it was so overwhelming, and—"

"I thought I'd made a huge mistake," I said, tears of relief welling in my eyes. I gestured to the big open living room. "I thought I'd misread every signal. The last two weeks, I thought—I thought—"

"I shouldn't have lied to you," she said. "I couldn't keep lying to you. I'm sorry. I'm so, so sorry."

"Damnit," I said. "Damnit, damnit, damnit."

"I'm sorry," she said again.

"Not you," I said. "My mother. She set me up. She— she—"

"She didn't make either of us do anything. She can't make us." She paused. "I can leave if you want me to."

"I love you," I said.

"I love you," Mel said. "Nobody can make me do that."

"I suppose not," I said. I knew it wasn't her fault. My mother had set me up, and Melanie was no more to blame than I was. Here we were, two pawns in the same game. And who else on this planet could possibly understand how that felt?

We developed a weekend routine. Saturdays we did chores, laundry, grocery shopping, scrubbing the bathroom, raking up pine needles. We saw my parents on Saturday nights; dinner was at their house at six o'clock sharp. Sundays in the morning we relaxed with the paper; in the afternoon, we sat at opposite ends of the dining table and spread our work out. It was a good time for thinking, for moving things around in a way I didn't in my lab, for contemplating things I might otherwise not have conceived.

This particular Sunday, mid-October, it was chilly outside, and Melanie had made a pot of coffee. It sat between us on the table. She drank more of it than I did; I would drink a cup in the morning sometimes, but mostly I just liked to hold the warm cup between my hands. The cups had come from my parents' house, a medium blue, speckled with white, not quite big enough to hold comfortably with both hands around them. I had three articles stacked in front of me that had collected on my desk during the week. Mel had papers everywhere, little crumpled scraps, a looseleaf notebook, xeroxes of journal articles, extending past the table's midline. She seemed to know what they all were and where, reaching for one without looking up to search, keeping notes on a yellow pad resting in her lap.

She had just refilled her coffee cup and was settling back into her chair when the doorbell rang. We looked at each other.

"Beats me," I said. "Want me to get it?"

"I'll get it." Her end of the table was closer to the door. She opened the door and I expected voices, an introduction, a request from whoever was standing there, but instead there was silence. I couldn't see the door from where I sat.

"Mel?" I called. "Who is it?"

"Who are you?" came a voice. A voice I knew. In an instant I was up. Celine was standing there in a thin black sweater.

"What are you doing here?" I asked. I looked down at my hands, sure that they must be shaking, but they appeared still. Cold air was pouring into the house. She gave no answer. Melanie was still standing beside me, looking at her. Somehow I was supposed to introduce them. Neither knew the other existed. No, I thought, that wasn't completely accurate. Celine had known about Melanie, the Melanie in my past, her only predecessor of any note.

"Celine," I said, "this is Melanie. Mel, Celine is—we knew each other before I came back. In Boston."

"You're going to freeze out there," Melanie said. She moved aside, gesturing for Celine to come in. I stood dumbly, feeling that I couldn't explain to either one of them about the other; that would entail a clear establishment of allegiance. Seconds ticked by.

"Well," Melanie said. "I've got to run some of these things back over to the lab."

"Wait," I said. My heart was racing. "Mel—"

"We can talk later," she said. She held my gaze for several seconds. Her eyes were soft; she meant it. She disappeared back into the kitchen to gather her things, and all I could think in that moment was how incredibly kind she was. She was everything anyone had ever wanted for me.

It wasn't until after Melanie brushed past us, her arms full of the papers she'd had spread out over the table, and gone out the door, car keys looped over her pinky, that Celine spoke.

"I thought you'd be alone," she said. My heart was still beating much too fast. I wouldn't have thought, if anyone had asked, that her appearance would send me into such a state.

"We can't just stand in the hallway like this," I said.

"Mel," she said. "Melanie. Jesus, was that her? The one?" I nodded. Celine hadn't moved from where her feet were planted in the entryway. I could see that she was constructing a narrative in her head, one in which, rather than the job being irresistible, I had engineered this entire thing for the sake of reunion, behind her back. "And you're apparently still in love with her."

Her anger shook me, and at the same time the intimacy of it plunged me into memory, the two of us talking by the Charles, her elegant signature right above mine on a lease.

"No." I said. "You have to believe me. I didn't know she lived here. I hadn't spoken to her in years and years."

"Oh," she said. "How convenient." She towered over me in high heels.

"You don't believe me," I said. "You think I left my brilliant, beautiful girlfriend and my work in Boston to come home and be with my high school sweetheart."

"I don't know," she said. She sniffed.

"What are you doing here?" I asked.

"I'll go. I should have just called you. I should never have come."

"Stay," I said. "Please." I took her hand and pulled her to the living room. My palms were hot. She was wearing lipstick, an orangey shade of red, and her skin was so clear it practically looked damp. I hadn't thought of her much in the last few months—I'd thought so much of my work, and of Mel—but now I couldn't see how that had been the case.

"I'm embarrassed," she said. "I came here thinking you'd be on your own, and you'd let me in, and we'd, well, I don't know, we'd figure it out." I gestured to the small sofa, and we sat, both rather formal with two feet planted on the floor, several inches of cushion between us. I could barely fit it all together, Celine in my living room in Los Alamos, Melanie and Celine standing next to each other, the cold air blowing in, it made no sense, like a dream where you know where you are and who the people represent but nothing actually appears the way it does in real life.

"I don't know what to say," I told her. "You said it yourself: There's nothing here for you. It was an either/or proposition."

"That's what he wanted you to think. Your dad. I wasn't part of his plan. So I'd just disappear, I'd fade into the background and you could go back to being Mr. Brilliant Child Prodigy Research Guy. Apparently with Ms. Brilliant Child Prodigy Research Girl for a wife. I just didn't think it was *you* that wanted it."

"It wasn't me," I said. "It was my mother. She convinced Mel to stay here after I took the job. I didn't know anything about it. I didn't even know she was back until I got here. I swear, I had no idea."

She laughed, an insincere cackle. "Of course your mother arranged it. I'm not even surprised. Sweet Christ, Curt, doesn't that make you mad?"

"Yes," I said. My voice cracked on the word. I wanted to put some force behind my words, to yell, but I could barely get the sounds out; my throat ached. "Of course it does. I hate that she did it, behind my back like that."

"You don't have to put up with it," Celine said. She laid a hand on my arm. "God, I hate to see you like this. You can shake it off, Curt. You can break out of it." She leaned in and locked her blue eyes on mine. "You can do this," she said. "I know you can."

"She just wanted me to be happy." I said. A tear slid down my right cheek. "And she wanted Mel to be happy."

"Never mind what *you* want."

I didn't answer. What did I want? I couldn't have said. We *were* happy, in a way. We had good jobs, and a comfortable house. We were well matched.

"What would happen if you confronted her?" Celine asked. "If you went over there and knocked on the door, and said Mom, why on earth did you interfere in my life this way, please don't ever do that again?"

"She'd tell me that Dad wanted me to be successful, and she wanted me to be happy, and they tried their best to make that happen."

"So you tell her thank you, Mom, that's sweet, but I'm an adult now and it's my life, and please don't."

"I can't," I said. "I can't do that." She gave a violent sigh and closed her eyes.

"I'll go, then," She said. She stood. "I'm terribly sorry. I hope I didn't just ruin your marriage."

"Don't go," I said. It was all I could think, in that moment—I didn't want her to go. A feeling had started to stir in me that I hadn't felt since my return. It was different, *I* was different, and I knew as she stood there, tears welling in her eyes, that whatever it was, I wouldn't have it here, not without her, not ever again.

"I'm going to Paris for the year," she said. "And I—God, I'm such an idiot. I did some research, and asked around, and there's a lab there where they're working in your area, and I really thought there was a chance that you'd come." She cast her eyes around the house, the table where Mel and I had been working, the two sets of shoes lined up neatly by the door. They fit perfectly there. I thought of my lab, the window sill with its line of houseplants in mismatched pots.

"I need to think," I said.

"No," she said, "you don't. It's all you do, think, think, think.

Just come. Please just for once in your life, just come with me right now." I wasn't getting enough air into my lungs.

"I can't," I said.

"You mean you won't."

"I can't," I said again, but I knew she was right. It was all there, the data to support the conclusion: they had set me up, the pair of them, and comprehending this, and that it had always been so, I stood, watching the only person who had ever stood a chance of pulling me out get into a rental car and drive away.

I called Mel's office. "She's gone," I said. "Mel, I didn't ask her to come." The line was silent for a long time. "Are you there?"

"Okay," she said.

"I mean it," I said. "We split up when I left Boston, and I hadn't heard from her."

"I believe you," she said. Her voice was tiny, far away. Then, "She's very tall."

"Yes," I said, "too tall, much too tall."

"Are you in love with her?" Melanie asked.

"Oh, Mel," I said, "what does it matter?"

ADAM BROOKS, 1957

It isn't that they'd been expecting a grand welcome—the lab is a busy place, their arrival a minor event—but there was no need for the guard at the gate to bark at them the way he did. They had their passes, carefully arranged ahead of time, and soon enough their station wagon would have a decal and the guards would come to recognize them.

Adam and Angeline are both frightened by the guard's rifle. He isn't exactly pointing it at them, but the angle at which he holds it suggests that a wrong move could prove fatal. Adam tries to steady himself, his hands tight on the wheel. Hundreds of scientists have come here before him, in times much more dire than these.

Once they are inside the gates, things seem a little calmer. There are streets with street signs, just like Iowa, just like Pasadena. They have been given directions to a particular office, where a woman they have spoken to on the phone, Mrs. Harding, will show them to their assigned unit, and later, when they've had a chance to settle in, give them a more complete tour.

The house is tiny; they can see that from the outside as they follow Mrs. Harding's car to the short gravel driveway. It is packed between two equally tiny houses that look like they came off a conveyor belt. It has just two rooms, a bedroom and a living room, each with a sad assortment of dormitory-style furniture, plus an impossibly small kitchen with a two-burner stove and a bathroom where two people cannot stand side by side. There is a large round stain on the carpet in the bedroom, right at the foot of the rickety bed, and everywhere the paint is flaking. Angeline puts one finger on the living room wall and pulls it away covered in fine, white dust.

"You'll be able to move," Mrs. Harding says apologetically. "They're continuing to build new structures, and as people move out, spaces open up." Adam looks around at the dim rooms, the stain. He looks at his new wife, her forehead wrinkled, her lips pressed stoically together. It is late afternoon, the sky already pink-orange.

"Thank you," he says to Mrs. Harding, positioning himself between her and the doorway that leads to the bedroom, giving her no choice but to edge toward the door. "What time shall we come by in the morning for the tour?"

"How about ten o'clock?" she says. "You can get yourselves some dinner at the lodge tonight. It'll open up at five. Do you know where it is?"

"We'll find it," Adam says.

When she's gone, he takes his wife in his arms. "Don't worry," he says. "These are quarters for the new man. And damned if anybody will call me junior for more than a couple of months."

"We can make do," she says, bravely. Her voice suggests that she doesn't believe it herself, and he can't blame her. She goes to the tiny, chipped sink in the kitchen and turns on the tap; she washes the dust off her hands as best she can. She is hunting around for something on which to dry her hands when there is a forceful knock at the door. She draws in a great breath through her nose, a sign Adam has come to recognize that she is trying to gather her composure.

He opens the door, prepared to accept some piece of paperwork or additional unwanted advice from Mrs. Harding, hoping to run her off quickly so he can be alone with Angeline, but it isn't Mrs. Harding. It is a tall man with silver hair combed straight back from his face. He wears a jacket and tie.

"Dr. Brooks," he says. "I'm sorry I couldn't meet you at the gate. I was tied up on a phone call to Washington. I'm Norris Bradbury." Adam's mouth falls open. Dr. Bradbury is the head of the laboratory, successor to Oppenheimer, responsible for keeping the lab going now that the immediate urgencies of war have passed. He hadn't imagined he'd meet him at all in the early stages of his work here.

Dr. Bradbury offers his hand. "Welcome," he says. "Welcome, welcome, welcome. I think, I do believe, that you will learn to feel at home here quickly."

Adam turns to Angeline, who looks stunned. She wipes her hands on her skirt, and Adam introduces her. Dr. Bradbury smiles.

"Don't you worry," he says. "We'll get both of you into a nicer place just as soon as we can. Adam, I was hoping I could bring you over to the technical area. Just for an hour or so, show you a few things, get the last bit of paperwork squared away so we can hit the ground running tomorrow."

"Well," Adam says. "You don't waste any time." He looks at Angeline, her lips set once again in that tight line. She gives the slightest of nods.

"Go," she says. "Do what needs to be done." This is not the first time she has told him this, and it won't be the last, and he loves her for it. Good God, he loves her.

CEILING

It was never her plan to hide the letter. It was on Thursday that she opened the mailbox to find the big white envelope, postmarked Pasadena, addressed to Curtis. They had been expecting this—an acceptance from the California Institute of Technology—any day. She didn't know who had been more anxious, her son, who would go there, or her husband, who had already been. She brought the envelope inside and set it on the kitchen table, propped against the salt shaker so there would be no missing it.

It wasn't yet two o'clock, and the house was quiet. She wasn't used to being home so much, but she'd had her gall bladder out the week before, and had been instructed not to return to work for a full two weeks. It had been nice the first few days, padding around the one-story house in her socks, sitting in whichever room she liked, but she'd quickly come to look forward to Curtis's arrival home from school. His comings and goings gave shape to her days.

The good news, she decided, warranted a celebration. It would be nice for Curtis, for Adam, and perhaps the effort would help her to build the enthusiasm she knew she ought to feel. There was time to go to the store. There was time to make the lemon chicken Curtis loved, the dish she made for his birthday every year. She wasn't much of a cook, but this, she could do. Every time she served it, there was none left over. Those little tight smiles they gave when she cooked much of anything else were nowhere to be found.

She picked up the envelope. Every once in a while, Curtis came home early, some activity or another having been canceled, or some necessary piece of equipment left in his bedroom. She would hate for him to come home to an empty house, no one there to be a part of that scene that would be in his memory forever. She carried it with her and set it on the front seat of her car. It sat there in the thin April sunshine while she passed up and down the aisles, gathering the ingredients from the list she knew by heart.

These days, when Curtis wanted to impress his father, he read obscure books and wrote out complicated proofs that he left lying in conspicuous places, but it had started with backyard experiments. Adam worked long hours and some weekends at the lab, but Sunday afternoons were set aside for Curtis, who by the age of eight summarily refused to make any other plans for the day, no matter what Angeline offered.

Adam had always presented the projects—the combination of baking soda and vinegar to produce a bubbling froth, the construction of a homemade light bulb—as serious investigation. He gave Curtis a hard-bound lab notebook pilfered from work and taught him the art of record-keeping, always recording the date, the time, the location, the materials, always writing in ink. "This is one for the books," he'd say, leading Curtis out to the garage where he kept stashes of chemicals, spare electrical parts, batteries, tools.

Angeline wasn't sure that Curtis enjoyed these charades. He looked scared as he worked, and some Sunday nights, she heard him tossing in bed late into the night. She imagined him worrying about the outcomes of the crucial experiments in which he believed his father was relying on him. It was too much for such a young boy. She brought him watercolor paints and thick, smudgy sticks of charcoal. She talked to him about the books he was reading in school and offered to drive him to friends' houses. She picked up the doodles he'd drawn in art class and praised them effusively. But if Adam was in the house, Curtis never seemed to hear her.

"Isn't this is getting out of hand?" She would ask Adam when the two of them had climbed into bed, the desk lamp still on after nine in Curtis's room down the hall. "He thinks he's taking the world on his shoulders."

"He's learning the importance of inquiry," Adam said. She turned toward him, but his eyes were locked somewhere far away. She knew his heart was in the right place, if he would ever admit to being guided by a heart, and it was true that she had no provable reason why her approach would be better, but she felt sure that she could convince him to go a little easier, that she should.

"He just wants to be around you," she said, as gently as she could. "He wants a little attention."

"I give him every Sunday." Still, he did not face her. He sat very straight against the headboard, his legs straight out, his toes sticking up under the quilt, with a perfect stack of three pillows. "That's more than Jim and Larry give their boys. Considerably more."

"I think, love," she said, "that he wants to know you think he's all right." She reached across the space between them and rested her hand gently on his forearm. He was in his nightshirt but still had his watch on.

"He is all right." He shifted on the mattress and turned his head even farther away, his eyes cast now to the corner of the room. "His notes are more meticulous than mine are. Any lab in the country will be able to use a kid like this."

"Tell him," she said. And Adam would nod, but she'd never heard him offer that kind of praise. Not to anyone.

Curtis had not come home when she arrived back at the house. She tucked the envelope under one arm as she carried her two plastic grocery bags into the house. It fell on the floor as she settled the bags on the counter. She considered how the rest of the afternoon would go. Maybe she should put the letter back in the mailbox. She could tell Curtis she'd been too busy, or had been resting, and ask him to go out for the mail. Or she could put it back on the table and wait for him to see. She wished all the colleges had replied at once. He would be accepted, she was sure, at Columbia, too, and Chicago. She could have laid the choices out in front of him, looking for the moment like paths that were equally open to him. She could have pretended, they all could have, that he might choose somewhere else, a school where he might discover other interests, where he would be more likely to meet people of the sort he had never come across here in Los Alamos.

She held it flat on the palm of her hand, feeling its heft, the cool smoothness of the paper. It was then, with two lemons rolling around on her counter, that it occurred to her that she could save it for a day or two. More letters would surely come, and soon. Rather than give it to him now, all of them assuming and agreeing that the choice was made, she could, for a little while longer, imagine that he might be more independent, more like her. But she had already bought the ingredients for the lemon chicken. Surely, even if she did not prepare it, Curtis would notice the contents of the refrigerator.

Still, the thought of just another day or two with uncertainty, with possibility, was attractive. She could see her husband's face, the mixture of smug I-told-you-so certainty and genuine pride that his son was so much like him, and she couldn't bear it. She carried the envelope down the hall to her bedroom.

She slid open the top drawer of her chest and scooped out her underthings: stockings, camisoles, bras, panties. She laid the envelope smoothly along the bottom. She piled her things hastily back in and returned to the kitchen, her cheeks flushed. She checked the kitchen clock. It was just after three. She still had perhaps half an hour before Curtis arrived. He would hate it if he knew she had planned a celebration before the news had come; she was going to have to make it into no celebration at all, a diversion she had dreamed up for herself to pass the restless hours. She set to work immediately; it would have to be well underway if it was supposed to be a project undertaken for its own sake during the long, lonely afternoon.

Soon she was chopping onions, juicing lemons, preparing to marinate the chicken. The big knife had gone dull. She had to saw back and forth on the onion to break through the skin. Once, the knife slipped, and for a moment she was so sure she had sliced through her finger that she stared in disbelief at her dry, white hand, searching for blood.

She was pouring the batter for a loaf of soda bread into a greased pan when he came through the door, backpack slung over one shoulder.

"Any mail?" he said.

"Nothing yet, darling." She hoped she sounded as she had on all the other days when she'd given the same answer. Curtis made a sound, a little cough. His face showed something more than the mild disappointment of waiting another day. "What's wrong?" she asked. She could feel her pulse in her neck, and in her thumbs.

"Clark Anderson got his today," Curtis said. "His mother called the school when the mailman came. Mrs. Ford came and got him out of class."

"All the schools are a little different, Sweetie," she said. "Just because one school mailed acceptances doesn't mean—"

"No, Mom, it was Cal Tech. If I'd gotten in, it would have come today." He kept his eyes down, and she felt a rush of sympathy. She knew how it felt to be too upset for eye contact, sure that what little composure was left to you would not withstand a moment's personal connection.

"Well now," she said, "the mail here has never been all that reliable."

"I want to call Dad," Curtis said. "I should tell him."

"Now hang on," Angeline said. "Let's not get ahead of ourselves. There's no reason to assume the worst." Her throat ached. She let the loaf pan sit unbaked on the counter, the oven hot, ready. She took a deep breath and tried to think. She could bring an instant end to his suffering. But if she produced the envelope now, it would seem like a cruel prank she had played on him, and then the evening would unfold between Curtis and Adam, as a celebration of Curtis's impending departure for Pasadena, and she couldn't bear to see his center of gravity shift already from here to there. She needed another day or two, the survival of a slim hope that he might surprise them all.

"The post office is fine," he said, his voice so soft it barely disturbed the air around him.

"No one is a better student than you," she said. "And with your connections. I'm sure it will be here any day. Maybe they're sending you a special letter, a special offer, and it took an extra day or two to put together."

"Yeah," he said, "maybe."

"I'm making us a special dinner," she said. "Just because I love you. Your favorite chicken."

"I don't want lemon chicken," he said. "I want to go to Cal Tech."

"I know you do, Baby," she said. "Why don't you get started on your homework. Take your mind off it. You want something to drink?" He didn't answer her. He disappeared down the hall into his room, and a minute later she heard the opening chords of "Tax Man," muffled by his closed door.

She put the bread into the oven. She was suddenly very tired. She sat in one of the hard kitchen chairs and rested her head in her hand. She hadn't had a day this active since before her surgery, and she had worn herself out. The smell of the bread started to permeate the air. She wondered if Curtis was thinking about the other schools he had applied to, if he knew which was his next choice, if there was any part of him, even some secret, silenced part, that might be relieved. She didn't imagine so; the sting of rejection would take a few days to give way to planning, and by then she'd have slipped the letter back in among the rest of the mail. "Tax Man" turned into "Eleanor Rigby." She wanted to lie down, but she didn't want to be in the bedroom, with the letter. She moved to Adam's easy chair in the living room and propped her feet on the ottoman. She closed her eyes, and dozed.

She didn't like these long lonely days. All afternoon she had been waiting for Curtis, and now that part of the day had come and gone in the space of a few minutes, and she was waiting for Adam. Lots of women, she knew, lived their entire lives like this, their lives shaped by the comings and goings of men. They must have had their own ways of arranging their days so that they weren't disappointed all the time. She wondered if this prospect was what had driven her own mother away. She had never before felt even a tiny grain of understanding of how she could have done it, disappeared, leaving a daughter who had not yet learned to walk, back to France without leaving so much as a photograph, trying for all the world to make it seem as though she had never been there.

But of course, she had been there, had loved a professor, or thought she had, had given birth to a restless daughter. And now Angeline herself felt that she was fading from the Earth, that her son might go off into the world stamped deeply, indelibly, with the marks of his father, like a newer, faster train along the same track that had been laid before he was born. And when he was gone, she, too, would vanish.

There had been one Sunday morning, during a particularly intense period in Adam's work on the Test Ban Treaty, when he'd sequestered himself in his study shortly after dawn. Angeline wasn't sure of the details, but she understood that Adam was trying to work out a very delicate deal, and she suspected that he was working outside of the rules, risking his own high position in hopes of preventing greater destruction. He had seen and imagined things she could not absorb. She was staying out of his way, nursing a cup of coffee and skimming the paper, when he burst into the hallway.

"Get away from here!" he roared. "You thought you'd eavesdrop on me? You want the FBI coming in here?" Curtis had been sitting, unobserved by either parent until that moment, outside the study door, waiting for his father to emerge and begin their usual Sunday time together. Instinctively, Angeline got to her feet and went to the doorway, where she could see Curtis shuffling backward toward his bedroom.

"I'm sorry," Curtis said faintly.

"Sorry doesn't mean anything!"

Curtis ran down the hall into his room, barely getting the door closed before he began to cry. Angeline knew better than to speak to Adam just then. She'd learned, through years of quiet observation, that more likely than not, he was afraid that he was in the midst of some monumental failure. He meant no harm. He had to be forgiven a slip of the temper here and there, with everything that he was trying to do. She went instead to Curtis's room.

"He didn't mean it, sweetie," she said, standing in the doorway. "He was mad at the man on the phone, and he took it out on you."

"I shouldn't have been there," Curtis said into his pillow. "I shouldn't have listened."

"Let's do something just you and me. I'll take you to town. Buy you a new comic."

"Leave me alone," Curtis said.

"I could take you over to the park and catch the baseball for you." He didn't answer. She stayed another minute, but he did not stir, and she withdrew. When she peeked in the door a few minutes later, he was hunched over a thick textbook, a gift from his father. *Introductory Physics,* Adam's own text from his first year at Cal Tech. It was far too difficult for even the brightest of twelve-year-olds, but Curtis could not be torn away.

That afternoon, Adam had gone to make amends. Angeline had been out in the garden when most of it had happened, getting everything ready for the winter, but she'd pieced it together well enough. Remorse had caught up with Adam, and he had planned an experiment for them to do together, a good one, a real treat. He'd found Curtis in his room, deep in his studies.

"I need your help," he said. Timidly, Curtis lifted his eyes but said nothing. "Know anything about sodium?"

"A member of the alkali family," Curtis said, barely above a whisper. "Atomic number twelve. No, eleven. Twelve."

"Eleven," Adam said, much more gentle than he usually was in correcting Curtis. "I have an investigation to conduct. Think you can give me a hand?"

"You don't want me," Curtis said. "You want someone who doesn't wait in the hall."

"I want you," Adam said. "You take the best notes."

Together, they went out to the garage, where Adam took a big metal box from a high shelf. The box contained a large, silvery-white lump of metal, packed in oil, and several smaller pieces.

They brought it into the house. Adam took a pasta pot from the rack on the wall and filled it with several inches of water as Curtis recorded all the information he had so far: *12/5/68. Los Alamos, NM. Sample of elemental sodium, source unknown.* His hand shook as he wrote, and he pressed harder to keep his letters even.

"What's the research question?" Curtis asked.

"Just watch a minute." Using a pair of Angeline's kitchen tongs, he took the smallest piece of sodium, no bigger than a raisin, and dropped it into the pot. Immediately, it began to sizzle and whiz, skipping across the surface of the water, glowing hot. It banged against the metal sides of the pot and sputtered and burned until it sank, reduced to a pebble of ash, and came to rest on the bottom.

"I see," Curtis said. "We can use it as a fuel."

"Exactly," Adam said. "We'll test some of these different pieces and see how they behave. That big one, though, we'll have to take to Ashley Pond. When the chunks reach a certain size, they don't just sizzle. They explode."

Curtis's eyes grew wide as he struggled for the proper response. "How are we going to measure the— the— the energy output?"

"So far, we're just observing," Adam said. "Once we get a sense of what we're dealing with, we can design a more controlled experiment." Curtis dropped the next piece in and watched it sizzle.

Adam did the third one. The sodium whizzed and clanged and smoked and burned.

The fourth piece was bigger than the first few. "Stand back," Adam warned. "This one might burn hotter."

"That's a good point," Curtis said. "There's no reason to assume a— a—" he struggled again for the words— "a linear correlation between size and energy output."

"Attaboy," Adam said. "Now stand back and let her rip." Curtis dipped into the metal box with the tongs, took the lump of sodium, and stood back.

Angeline heard the bang from across the yard: as soon as it hit the water, the sodium broke into a dozen tiny pieces and flew, in a shower of sparks, out of the pasta pot and high up to the ceiling. She came running inside to find her husband and her son staring at each other, a thin smoke in the air. It only took her an instant to look up and see the damage they'd done.

It was with characteristic force that, shortly after six, Adam came through the door. He was forever moving faster, and with more power, than was necessary, propelling himself from the bed to the shower, out the bathroom door after washing his hands, as though he were used to living in a world of more gravity than this one.

She watched him take in the array of bowls and pans that she hadn't yet cleaned. She could see his lightning-quick thought process. "News?" he asked.

"No news," she said. "I just had to get up and do something. A project."

"You're feeling better?"

"Yes" she said, "a bit."

"I'm glad to hear it." He leaned in and kissed her on the forehead.

"What kind of day was it?" she asked. This was another reason she hated being trapped at home. When she was at work, she could usually tell the tone of his day, even though she was up one floor and at the other end of the hall. Now, this last week, the man who came through the door at the end of the day might be whistling, or might be barely able to lift his feet under all the weight he bore, work he was forbidden to discuss. She rubbed her temple. Her secret was nothing, she knew, a tiny deception, a burden of her own making. But she felt it there between them.

"An uneventful day," he said. "On all fronts, it seems."

When the three of them sat down to dinner, Angeline found herself without anything to say. Any mention of colleges would require a lie. The clinking of silverware grew heavy in the air. She considered turning on the radio for a newscast, but Adam didn't like to listen to the news at home. It made him tense and irritable.

Finally, Curtis spoke. "Clark Anderson got into Cal Tech today. Mom thinks my letter is still coming. Delayed at the post office, or mailed separately. I think that's unlikely." He put a very large piece of chicken into his mouth and chewed intently. His eyes were fixed somewhere over Adam's head.

"Today?" Adam said. "The letter came today?"

"His mother called the school." Adam looked at Angeline for confirmation, or perhaps for some clue as to what all this meant. She pressed her lips together. He had been certain that Curtis would be swiftly admitted, more certain than the rest of them. He would know that something wasn't right.

"Well," Adam said at last, "I'm sure your mother's right."

"There's more bread," Angeline said. "Would anyone like more bread? I could make more salad if anyone—"

"I'm not hungry," Curtis said. He turned to Adam. "May I be excused?"

"All right," Adam said. "But thank your mother for making you this wonderful dinner."

"Thank you," Curtis said, his back already half turned as he retreated to his room. Angeline bit the inside of her mouth. She knew it wasn't so, it couldn't be so, but it felt as though Curtis were blaming her, as though he had intuited that it was her fault, that she had the power to fix it.

"Don't take it personally," Adam said when they'd heard the door to Curtis's room click shut. "He's seventeen. He's upset. The chicken is delicious."

"I'm sure he'll have a whole slew of offers," Angeline said. "They'll come all at once. By the end of the week, five or six."

"Yes," said Adam, "I imagine so."

"I still think it's coming," she said. She was aware of the silky fabric of her blouse on her skin, of the clasps of her bra on her back.

"Are you really feeling better?" Adam asked. "You seem tired. Maybe you overdid it today."

"Maybe I did," she said.

"I'll give you a hand with the dishes." The two of them were still at the sink when Curtis came out again, his arms full of books.

"I'm going next door," he said. Angeline drew a breath, intending to impose some limit. Melanie, the neighbors' daughter, was a year older than Curtis but the same grade in school. As they'd grown, they had become formidable competition for one another, and then powerful allies, and now, though Curtis refused to discuss it, obviously something more. The slow evolution had made it difficult to draw the lines she otherwise would have drawn. But Curtis looked miserable and this was the only thing that seemed like it might offer comfort.

"Have a good time," she said. Her voice cracked on the last word. She turned back to Adam. He had put down his dish towel and was staring at the reflection in the kitchen window. "What is it?" she said.

"That Anderson boy," Adam said. "You know perfectly well our post office is as good as any other."

"I'm sure it's nothing," she said. "He must have gotten in. You were so certain."

"I'm never certain of anything," Adam said. "None of us is."

"It wouldn't kill him to consider some other options," she said.

"Even if he does end up in Pasadena."

"I just don't understand," Adam said. "With me, and your father, and his grades, and all the work he's done. I just don't see how it could have happened."

"He'll be accepted," Angeline said. "I think he'll go. I've just got a feeling."

"You've got a feeling," Adam said. "That's wonderful." Abruptly, he sat down, right there on the kitchen floor. It took a moment for Angeline to realize what was happening; she had never seen it before. Her husband was crying.

When she'd first seen, that fateful Sunday, what had happened to her ceiling, she let Adam have it. "You moron," she said. "You could've burned the house down!" There were a few other names she would've liked to call him, but not in front of Curtis.

"I miscalculated," Adam said, "I'll admit. I'm not a chemist."

"Clean it up," she said, leaving dangerous pauses between each word.

"I'll clean it up," Curtis said. "I was the one who dropped that piece in."

"No, sweetie," Angeline said. "Your father started this mess. He should've known better."

"We were working on it together," Curtis insisted. "Researching new fuels." And just as Angeline was about to refuse a second time, she saw Adam, out of the corner of her eye, draw a finger quickly across his throat.

But Curtis, infinitely more perceptive than his father, had seen. "What did you just do?" he said. "Dad?" But Adam didn't have to answer. Curtis had understood everything in an instant, understood that it was his father telling his mother to let him pretend, because the experiment was all a sham, part of a carefully calculated program designed to make him feel like the adult that he clearly was not. He had been betrayed, and he was wounded to the core. He took the pot, still cloudy with burned sodium, and flung it to the floor by Adam's feet. Angeline yelped and jumped back.

"Liar," Curtis said. His sweet face, the face with Adam's chin, was red and crumpled. Secretly, silently, Angeline cheered him on. She would catch him gently. She would reward him.

Adam, backed into a corner, shifted his stance. He had processed the situation, all the possible resolutions, in the space of three seconds. "I apologize," he said. "You've outgrown it. You want to be an adult now?" Curtis didn't answer, but Adam barreled on. "Here's your first real adult assignment. No kid stuff. You clean up this kitchen. Get it perfect. I don't want to see that there were ever any scars on that ceiling." Curtis looked around the room, tears streaming. He looked up at the ceiling, ten feet above, and down at the floor. "Quit crying," Adam said. "I mean it. You're an adult now." To Angeline's horror, Curtis drew one more shuddering breath, then got down on his knees and began soaking up the water with a towel.

Angeline could not bear it. She had to intervene. "You don't need to do this, sweetie," she said. "Let's go for a ride. We'll get an ice cream. You've done enough."

"I can do it," Curtis said. "I can fix the ceiling."

"Leave it," Angeline said, her voice rising. "Adam, let him be. Curtis, you get up off that floor right now." But even as she spoke, she realized what her insistence had set in motion: Curtis ran straight to his father, leaving her there with her hand outstretched.

"Wait here a minute," Angeline said to Adam, with her greatest tenderness. With speed, with lightness, she was in the bedroom, in the drawer, her hands among the silky things. She felt a rush of warmth for her husband. She left the drawer open a little, thinking they might return to it once the air was clear. Then she was back in the kitchen, sinking to the floor beside him.

"I didn't mean to keep this from you," she said. She touched his damp cheek. He didn't understand what it was. He was still crying, not sobbing, but hiccuping, trying to get ahold of himself. "See?" she said. "He got in. He'll go, if that's what he wants. You did it." He took the envelope, still sealed.

"Where did you get this?" he asked, as though he didn't quite believe it was real.

"It came in the mail," she said. "I kept it with me when I went to the store, so he wouldn't come home and find it without us, and then I— I—"

"I've got to go tell him," Adam said. He got to his feet so quickly that Angeline had to step back to avoid the swinging of his arms.

"Wait," she said. "We can put it in the mailbox tomorrow. He'll get it. He'll be fine for tonight."

"What the hell were you thinking?"

"I just wanted another day or two," she said. "I thought maybe more would come, and if he had a different one first, he might really think about it. I've never done anything like this before. You know I haven't."

"You're torturing him," Adam said. The word hung between them for a moment. She thought of saying something about the comfort of their lives, about pain. They knew about suffering, both of them did, from their work, and this was not it. But Adam spoke first.

"This is the only thing he wants and now he thinks he'll never have it."

"I'm not sure it's what *he* wants," Angeline said. She wanted to say more but she held her tongue. Adam was already on his way out the door, storming across the yard, envelope in hand. He didn't even bother with the road; he cut straight through the pine trees that separated their yard from the Driscolls'. She wanted to go after him, but this had been coming for years, and she had allowed it. Now she could no more stop it than she could split an atom with her bare hands.

ANGELINE BROOKS, 1958

HIS HAND IS UNDER her nightgown, tugging at the elastic of her underpants.

"Stop," she says. "Adam, stop." He does not stop. His other hand is there now too, tugging, sliding them down her hips. His breath is hot on her neck. She hadn't awakened when he came in, does not know what time it is. His chin is rough against her neck.

She lies still another minute as he works the fabric down to her knees, summoning her strength, then gives a great twist, all her strength focused on this one movement, to the far side of the double bed.

"At least let me get the diaphragm," she says. She sits up. The window behind the bed is open a few inches. A breeze comes in, smelling of smoke, raising goosebumps on her arms. Somewhere not too far from here, she has heard on the radio, a fire is raging its way through the pine forests.

"You don't need to," he says. She gasps without meaning to, without realizing it was coming.

"We haven't thought this through," she says. "I'm not sure."

He sits up beside her and snaps on a light.

They have been at the lab for a year, gotten settled into a better house. There are other young families among them, a daycare, an elementary school.

"Do you think we're all going to still be here in a couple of years?" she says. An owl hoots somewhere out in the yard. In the dim light, she spies a cobweb high in the corner, stretching halfway down the wall.

"In New Mexico?"

"Come on, Adam. You must think about this." She reaches down and pulls her underpants back up to her waist, then smooths the nightgown back down around her legs.

"Of course there's a chance," he says. She looks him straight in the face. And there they are, the tiny lines at the corners of his eyes that appear when he is really worried, not about bills, or pneumonia, but about the End. She imagines she is the only one in the world who can see that sign, who knows what it means. He again extends a hand but she shrinks back, her right leg off the edge of the bed now, her foot anchored to the floor. "We really have to talk about this now?"

"I can wait," she says. "I can wait as long as you want."

"Listen," he says, "I really don't think this will be a problem. I've thought it through."

"You can't just think it through yourself and pronounce it done," she says. "This is a decision for two people to make together. We've got to talk about it. We've got to agree."

"Well, what do you want to know?" he says. "We've got nuclear weapons. The Soviets have nuclear weapons. It is within the realm of possibility that we, or they, will use them. They are massively destructive. Many, many times the power of the ones used in Japan. And we are still here on this planet orbiting the sun with lives to live."

"We couldn't protect a child from that," she says. "The world has never been like this before."

"There are people all over the country having children at a rate we've never seen before. You know what they're calling it, don't you? The Baby Boom?"

"But they don't know what we know," Angeline says. "They only know what's in the papers."

"So they can't prepare the way we can."

"We'd have to build a shelter," Angeline says. "We could set aside everything we would need. Tell me. Be honest. Could we make it safe?"

"Reasonably so," he says. He reaches across the bed, puts a hand on her hip. "There would be a problem, though."

"With building a shelter?"

"If we have a shelter," he says, "a real one, a good, safe one, and we have it stocked with supplies that would allow us to survive for some time—"

"Which we would need," she says, "if we were to do this. Enough for three." Instinctively, she puts her hand to her abdomen.

"Yes," he says. "But if we had such a thing, and others did not."

"Oh," she says. "Oh, lord. Could we turn them away? We couldn't. Adam, we couldn't."

"And yet if we didn't," he says, "how long could we last? We build it for three, or for four, and suddenly we've got twenty."

"Or we've killed seventeen."

"It's very late," he says. "It's nearly four." He switches off the light. She stays propped up beside him, trying to make out the shape of the cobweb on the ceiling in the darkness. The breeze keeps blowing, colder now on her bare skin. She realizes that a part of her had wanted him to try again; he doesn't often touch her, and she feels now, with this talk of explosions, of mortality, a deep physical need. Adam begins to snore lightly, and she wonders how he can sleep.

VELOCITY

She had been trying to get to the lab. This was the first thing Melanie remembered. She realized where she was almost instantly, without opening her eyes: it was the smell and the sound of a hospital, the same hospital where she had spent the night two Aprils before when her appendix had nearly burst. Upon opening her eyes she thought it might even be the same room, its tiny window, its curtain down the middle.

She had been trying to get to the lab, and now she was here. She must have fallen from her bicycle, or been thrown. Something was wrong with the right side of her body. A dull ache ran the length of her arm. A sensation more like an itch encircled her leg, which she realized was in a cast. Breath was painful.

She felt sure that something terrible had happened. Not the accident, but that something had been lost, something in her life altered. She couldn't remember what had happened, what had changed, but the dread was clear as day.

And where was Dean? She missed his big, gentle hands. It occurred to her that she might have been here a long time; it could have been days. He could have come and gone, waited, then gone again. She felt around for the button that had been beside her bed the last time she was here. It was right where she expected it to be. She pressed it.

"She's awake!" the nurse said brightly as she swept into the room. She looked young, perhaps not even yet Melanie's age, her long hair tied in a ponytail, freckles on her cheeks. "How are you feeling, Ms. Driscoll? Or shall I say Dr. Driscoll?"

"I feel fine. How long have I been here?" As she asked, it started to come back to her. She had defended her dissertation. Somebody—Dean—must have explained that to the nurse.

"Just since last night," the nurse said. "Your friend was here most of the night, the big fellow."

"My fiancé. Where did he go? What time is it now?" Why had he left her here? It wasn't like him. After the appendix, she'd had to shoo him out the door of their apartment so that she could get a little time on her own to think.

"It's just about noon. We can get a phone in here if you'd like to call him. Do you have any memory of the accident?"

"No," Melanie said.

"It was a pick-up truck that hit you. That's what the witnesses said. Fled the scene. Last I heard, they were still looking for him. All in all I'd say you were lucky. Lucky and smart, to have that helmet on."

"What's wrong with me? What did I break?"

"Two ribs, tibia, and patella, plus a pretty nasty bump to the shoulder and elbow. But it looks like everything's going to heal without surgery. How's the pain?"

"I don't feel much."

"Well you let us know if it starts to wear off. The doctor should be by around two." And the nurse was gone, ponytail swinging.

The defense had not gone as she'd expected. They would give her the degree—they did not allow students to schedule a defense if they weren't ready—but the questions had been more pointed than she had anticipated. One of the committee members in particular, a professor she didn't know well, had a set of concerns about her research that she had not considered. And worse, she realized as he spoke that he was right. She had been so occupied with writing down his comments that she had nearly failed to respond to his questions.

Dean had smiled at her from his seat at the edge of the room. He had smiled the whole time, easily visible over the heads of the other spectators, with his height, his hair that had grown long this last year, grazing his shoulders. As soon as the program had concluded, he'd descended on her, all hugs and congratulations, and she had wondered, had he not heard the same exchange that she had? Had he not recognized the deep incompleteness that one of the committee members had identified in her work?

"Hold your horses," she told him as he folded her into his arms, where she could practically disappear. "I've still got a lot of work to do." The hallway where they stood dead-ended, and she had her back to the corner. People were milling around outside the classroom where the presentation had been. The defense had been better attended than most, as she'd known it would be. She was, everybody knew, the best student they had. She wanted them to go away. She wanted to change out of this itchy blouse and get to work, thinking through the implications of the questions that had been raised. She did not want to shake hands, or accept congratulations. She did not want to talk about it.

"They're going to give you the degree," Dean said. "Didn't you hear the other three committee members? Full of praise."

"I don't want praise. I want to get it right."

Dean fumbled in his pocket where he used to keep his cigarettes before they'd both quit three months before, then drew his hand back out, still empty.

"Please," he said. "At least we can celebrate this step. A few letters after your name. It doesn't have to be about the dissertation."

"I'll catch up with you later," she said, already picturing herself in her tiny office off the lab, her feet tucked up under her, her favorite green pen. "I'll be home by ten, I promise."

"Oh no no no no," he said. "The least you can do is pretend to have fun with me. Just for a couple of hours."

"Keep your voice down," she said, eyeing the cluster of people ten feet down the hall, her advisor, the head of the department, students she saw and worked with every day. There were some younger students there, even some undergraduates, she thought, who might have been in one of the classes she'd had to teach. She knew she had developed a reputation in the department as the one to watch, and this made her even more ashamed. She had not lived up to it.

"I'm taking you to dinner," Dean said. "It's already arranged. We can't cancel it."

And so she had gone with him to the expensive restaurant where he had reserved a big table at the back. He had invited their downstairs neighbors, his coworker and wife whom they'd had to dinner a few times, people from her lab (although only a few had come, and not, she thought, the ones whose work and opinions she admired). He had ordered wine, and everybody had asked how it went and he'd told them that it was brilliant and perfect and interesting, which it wasn't, and they'd all raised glasses to her and the whole time she'd just been thinking of the critique Dr. Crawford had offered, and how spot on it was, how the hole he'd identified was a real one that might require her to rethink a larger portion of the dissertation than she had thought at first, wishing someone had brought it up sooner rather than simply cheering her on. The longer she waited to get it fixed, the later it would be when she moved on to the next project, and the fewer great projects there would ultimately be over the course of her finite lifetime.

But instead, she was here in this restaurant, with Dean and all these other people. It was kind of them to come and she didn't want to hurt their feelings, but with every bite she thought of what she would do next, how far she might be able to get before she had to take the manuscript to the binder who would make a copy that would stay forever in the department, before she had to walk for her diploma and vacate the lab she'd occupied for the last five years.

There were twelve of them. They filled three tables pushed together, and Melanie was wedged in the middle with her back to the wall, stiff in the new blouse and skirt she'd worn, her hair pulled back in a painfully tight twist. They hadn't ordered entrées; the table was instead strewn with dips and appetizers and salads, everything infused with garlic, half-empty wine bottles. The waitress had had to take away the flower arrangements and the candles to make room for all the glasses, the food.

Dean was to her left, and across from her, two men from her lab, Keith, who worked on chromatography, and Ollie, who had come from Germany and was obsessed with the idea of using microwaves for synthesis. Dean had always liked the two of them; they had invited him, once, to a poker night, where he'd lost a decent sum of money but come home laughing.

Ollie was telling a long story about something that had happened in Germany, but Melanie couldn't process the words. All the chatter was beginning to sound like gibberish. She tried to focus on the walls of the restaurant. There were big paintings of isolated body parts. Near the door was an ear. Over by the bar, a nose, and an elbow, and a thumb. It felt as though the dinner had gone on for hours.

"Hamburgers," someone was saying. "Definitely hamburgers." The chatter around the table was becoming unbearable. She needed the cool, clean comfort of quiet numbers on a page, equations that could be solved, results predicted.

She slid her chair back and set her napkin on the table. "Thank you all," she said, although only those closest to her could possibly have heard.

"Come on, Mel," Dean said. "We agreed. Just take this one night off. Have some wine."

"I can't," she said. Blood was roaring in her ears. She couldn't focus her eyes. She wound her way through the restaurant, squeezing past chairs that seemed perfectly placed to impede her progress. When she reached the sidewalk she took a gulp of air.

Then Dean was beside her. "Hey," he said. "You're okay. Deep breath." It was cool outside, and a little damp. The front windows of the restaurant were fogged up.

"I just want a few hours," she said. "Just to start thinking this through."

You can't leave now," he said. "Everyone came for you."

"You don't understand," she said. "I've got to figure this out."

"You can start revising first thing tomorrow. I'll make you a pot of coffee."

"It can't wait. It's fresh in my mind. I think he's right, you know, Crawford."

"The guy in the checked shirt?"

"Yes. It's running over and over in my head and I can't take any more chatter."

The traffic light changed, and the cars on the street beside them began to move. Somewhere in the distance a police siren wailed.

"It will still be there tomorrow," he said. "Hell, you can do it two hours from now. But you've got to come back in."

"I can't," she said. Tears were forming, and her nose began to itch. "I've got to fix it. I've got nothing, Dean. All I've got is a theory with a big fat hole in it." She sniffed and put a finger to the corner of her eye, trying to keep the tears in.

"Don't do this, Mel," he said. "Come back in. For me."

"This is who I am," she said. "You know that. You've always known that."

"Look, I ordered a cake," he said. "With your name on it and everything. I had to bring it over in the afternoon, before I came to the defense. Please, just come in while they bring it out, and have a piece, and then you can go."

"I don't know why you did that," she said.

"You want me to go back in there and eat it with all of your friends without you? Keith and Ollie and everyone is in there, and I don't think anybody would say they aren't good chemists who are going to have good careers because they came to a party one night."

"I'm not Keith and Ollie," Melanie said. "Thank you for doing this, Dean. It was sweet of you. Good night."

"Don't," he said.

She started walking.

"I mean it. I've put up with it every night for three years, but this is too much."

"This isn't about you," she said. "It's not like I'm going to be with some other man."

"If you keep walking, that's it." His jaw was clenched, his hands thrust deep in his pockets.

She remembered feeling certain that, if there was a choice to be made, she knew what she was choosing, that it was absolutely correct, that the mere act of requiring her to make such a choice was betrayal enough to dictate the outcome.

And so she had gone. This much, she remembered. She'd gone back to their apartment, where she had changed into jeans and collected her bicycle. She remembered carrying her bicycle down the stairs, remembered that her right hip had felt stiff when she'd swung a leg over the bicycle's frame, stiff from hours with her knees crossed during the defense. She remembered switching on the blinking headlight in the lingering dusk as she set off.

There was her dread: a dissertation needing to be pulled apart and stitched together. And Dean, suddenly objecting to the same priorities she had always had, wounded by them. His words stayed in her mind: *That's it.* She longed to go back to the moments when she'd first awakened, with only the dull, opiated ache in her broken bones.

She shifted in the bed, taking stock. The leg was in a cast from mid-calf to mid-thigh, slightly bent. Her elbow was wrapped in a soft bandage. She tried to move the arm and a shot of pain ran through her shoulder. With her other arm she reached up to feel her head; it felt normal, no scrapes or bumps or bandages. Gingerly she felt along her torso. Each breath brought a dull stab of pain; she wondered which two ribs were broken. Her head was not clear. She looked up at the IV pole beside the bed, the tube snaking down into her right arm, but she couldn't read its label without twisting to the right, and when she tried, the pain made her gasp involuntarily. Whatever it was, it was making her sleepy.

Someone was squeezing her arm gently, waking her. It wasn't Dean. It was a woman, a doctor, wearing glasses with green plastic frames.

"Is it two already?" Melanie said. "The nurse said you wouldn't be here until two."

"It's two-thirty," the woman said. "I'm Dr. Kerrigan. How are you feeling?"

"Where's Dean?" Melanie asked. "My fiancé."

"I'll ask them to check. Now, you took quite a spill." The doctor set about examining her, explaining the injuries as she went, asking her about pain, did this hurt, any pain here, but Melanie was focused on Dean. She knew there was a reason why she wasn't sure he was coming, but she couldn't remember. Then, she did remember, and her breath caught in her chest.

"Pain?" the doctor asked.

"No," Melanie said. "Not really."

"Well, it looks like you're going to heal up just fine," the doctor said. "I'd like you to stay one more night but if everything stays how it looks now, I see no reason why you couldn't go home in the morning."

"Is there a phone I can use?" Melanie asked.

They brought the phone in more quickly than she'd expected. She dialed the number of her lab, where she knew they would take her call. It rang six times before someone answered.

"It's Melanie," she said. "Who's this?"

It was a second-year student, and not one she knew very well.

"Listen," she said, "I was in an accident and I'm in the hospital and I'm okay, but I could really use something to read. Do you think there's someone there who might run something over for me?"

"Of course," the student said, as Melanie had known she would. They all regarded her as minor royalty, something more than a colleague, something different from Bob Franklin, the old professor who ran their lab, and she liked that. She knew it was earned. When they hung up she closed her eyes in relief. But the relief at the prospect of work only lasted a minute. The dread was still there. She closed her eyes, took a breath, and dialed Dean at his office.

"You're awake," he said. "How are you feeling? Are you in pain?"

"I can't tell," she said. "I think they've got me on enough drugs to eliminate any possibility of accurate perception."

"I'll come over," he said. "I'm sorry I couldn't be there when you woke up. They told me you were going to be fine, you just needed to rest. I came to work."

"It's fine."

"I'll be there as soon as I can."

"Dean, are we—did we—" He exhaled. She could see in her mind the way he was surely holding the phone, pressed between T-shirted shoulder and ear, the way he would be pulling on the fingers of his left hand with his right.

"Let's not talk about that now," he said. "Get some rest. Try to heal. See you soon." He hung up. She set the phone down and was overcome by nausea. She couldn't move, and there was nowhere to turn. Before she knew what was happening, she was vomiting, right onto herself, onto the bed, and the freckled nurse was back.

"Poor thing," the nurse said. "It's a common reaction to morphine. Out of the frying pan, into the fire. Let's get you cleaned up."

She must have slept, because she awakened. A man stood in the doorway to her room, but it wasn't Dean. It was John from her lab, Dean's opposite, short, with glasses and a shaved head. If there was anyone at the lab she would have considered a friend, she supposed John was it. He was a year behind her, his office two doors over. She had trusted him to read papers for her before she sent them out and always listened to his comments in their lab meetings. He hadn't been at the dinner; she supposed he had returned, sensibly, to the lab after the defense.

"Awake?" he said from the doorway. "Decent?"

"Both," she said. "Come in." She raised the back of the bed so she was sitting up.

He took a few steps toward her and stood, about even with her feet.

"So you drew the short straw?"

"I pulled rank," he said.

She smiled a little, involuntarily, at this bit of unfamiliar sweetness.

"Christ. Are you—"

"I'm apparently going to be fine," she said.

"Did it happen on the way home from the restaurant?" he asked. "When Ollie came in this morning he said you just kind of disappeared. I'm sorry I didn't come, by the way. I had time for either the defense or the party, and I thought you'd approve." She suddenly felt terribly exposed. Dean must have gone back in to that table full of people and served them her cake. She wondered if he'd made some excuse for her, pretended that he had acquiesced in her departure, a headache, an appointment he hadn't known of when he'd arranged the surprise. Or perhaps he had enlisted whoever among them might take his side in casting her as heartless. He was, she thought, just cruel enough to aim a barb at her as she departed, in a tone of jest with a core of truth.

"I was on my bike, on my way back to the lab."

"What a way to cap off the big day."

"Oh, it's probably fitting," she said. "I didn't see either one coming."

John laughed. "Well," he said, "I don't know about the bike, but with the defense, we all thought you were the one who would just talk for half an hour and they'd all bow and send you on your way. I don't think any of us saw it coming."

"I should have," she said. "I keep thinking I could have realized what was missing. I don't know how I didn't see it."

"Nobody else saw it either. It's like some secret genius dialogue between you and Crawford. I wish he'd talk to me like that. Where's your fiancé?"

"I guess he went to work," she said.

John raised an eyebrow. "How many bones did you break?"

"The nurse said he was here most of the night."

"I guess that's not my business," John said. "But it seems..."

"It serves me right," she said. "Punishment fits the crime. You don't need to stay, John. Weren't you trying to finish that asymmetric hydrogenation project this month? You're running out of time."

"Yes," he said, "I'll let you be. But first, I brought a few things." He took the plastic chair beside her bed. He smelled like coffee. He set a canvas tote bag down at his feet. From it he drew a copy of her dissertation, a new, blank spiral-bound notebook, two recent journals, and a yellow legal pad filled with writing. "My notes from your defense," he said. "I thought you, of all people, might be just masochistic enough to want them."

"You angel."

"I hope you're not discouraged," he said.

"No," she said, "not discouraged. Maybe frustrated. But I'd so much rather he tell me now, before it's really out there, while there's still a chance to fix it."

"Me, too," John said. "I never understand why people take these things so personally." John was a good chemist. He would do well. She thought she might still write to him, after she'd moved on to a post-doc, to wherever she would end up, and he, too, had found a place. She would still want to know what he thought.

"Dean doesn't understand," she said. "He thinks the point of this was, they're giving me the degree. Wahoo."

"He'll come around, don't you think? Wouldn't he rather be married to the woman who won the Nobel Prize than the woman who always sat next to him at dinner?"

"I don't know," Melanie said. "I thought so. I hope so." She regretted this last comment as soon as she'd said it. Three words too many. She was losing her composure.

"Maybe you're either born with it or you're not," John said.

"I don't know about that" Melanie said. "I came to it late. I had the most indulgent parents, growing up in New Mexico. It was like everything I did was a miracle to them. If I called them right now and told them I'd crashed my bicycle, they'd probably just go on about how I crashed it so brilliantly. All the injuries on one side of the body! Well done, daughter!"

"My parents were on the right side of that divide," John said. "Very strict. I hated it as a kid."

"Aren't you glad now, though?"

"I am. Though I wish it had been focused on a direction I could use. I took piano lessons, right up through high school. An hour of practice minimum per day. Our piano was in this strange little room, I think it was supposed to be a bedroom, and it took up the whole room, and they'd shut me in there and I couldn't come out for an hour. I tried bringing my homework in there a few times but my mother would come and pound on the door and ask why she couldn't hear any music." She tried to imagine John seated in front of a keyboard. All these years she'd worked with him and never known.

"Did you ever think you wanted to play? That you'd pursue it?"

"No," he said. "I wasn't any good at it. Although I'm sure it taught me discipline. And in a way, I kind of enjoyed it."

"Do you ever play now?"

"No," he said. "I haven't had access to a piano, really, since I left high school. But I wouldn't have time anyway. Have you ever heard of a pianist/chemist who actually managed to be any good at either?"

"I can't speak for music," she said, "but I can't imagine splitting the work we do with anything else that requires much in the way of time. I never had anything like that. My parents made me go to this awful camp where it was just, good job this, you're amazing that. Blue ribbons all around. Once, I tried doing things badly on purpose for a few days just to see if anyone would say anything. No one did."

"How old were you?"

"Nine or ten, I think. Then, I just started seeing it everywhere. Empty praise." She shifted on the mattress. The pillow had slipped from behind her head down toward her left shoulder. She couldn't use her injured right arm to reach it, nor could she twist to the side. She didn't want to ask John to move it, so she went on.

"I remember the first time anybody actually demanded something of me," Melanie said. "I was about to start sixth grade." Her voice sounded strange as she spoke, as though she were listening to someone else do an impression of her.

It had been terribly hot outside, summer in the desert. She was bored out of her mind. She was standing in the front yard, staring at the garage, staring at the swingset, when she smelled something smoky, like fireworks. She thought she knew where it was coming from. It was funny to remember; she knew these people much better now.

She was afraid of that next-door family. Curtis, the son, was in her class at school, but his father had some kind of big, important job, and never recognized her when they ran into each other in town. One time she saw him in the grocery store, near the meat counter, and he stared at her for at least a minute before silently turning and walking away. Later she always found herself peering around the corner by the butcher's to see if he was there.

She couldn't just go knock on their door and ask what they were doing and see if she could join. Instead she went around to the side of their yard. In place of a fence dividing the properties, there were tall pine trees, and Melanie was able to get underneath their low branches.

They were back there in the yard, Curtis and the father. She could hear them talking. They had a string tied to trees on opposite ends of their yard, cutting all the way across.

Curtis said, "We need all that speed going in the same direction."

"Speed and direction?" said Adam, the father. "What kind of words are those?"

Curtis sort of stammered for a minute, and then he said, "Velocity." Melanie thought she would've said "speed and direction," too, and gone on thinking it was correct forever. Her parents would've cracked open a bottle of champagne because she'd done something vaguely scientific-sounding.

She stayed there in the trees, watching them. They were doing some sort of experiment with different formulas for an explosive, using them to propel a little length of pipe along the string, trying to see which one would send it the farthest. She couldn't tell what the explosives were. It looked like sawdust, piled in newspaper cones. It was uncomfortable under there in the tree, with all the pine needles digging into her legs. She shifted, making too much noise.

"Who's there?" Adam shouted. "Show yourself." She stepped into the yard, thinking he would recognize her from next door, but he said, "Who are you, and why are you hiding in my pine trees?"

"It's Melanie," Curtis said. "From next door." Adam didn't seem embarrassed to not have recognized her.

"Well," he said, "get out or get to work." She didn't hesitate; she'd get to work.

"Miss Driscoll is going to be our measurement assistant," Adam said. He handed her a big old heavy tape measure, with a crank. He pointed to three cones of newspaper on the ground, each with a string snaking out of the bottom for a fuse, and said there were three forumlas, and they wanted the one that traveled the farthest.

Curtis had a lab notebook—she didn't recognize it at the time but of course that's what it was—and he was taking notes in tiny, meticulous handwriting. His father was looking over his shoulder. Then—and this surprised her more than anything—he passed Curtis a box of long fireplace matches. Curtis lit the string on one of the cones, and they all watched it burn for a few seconds, and then there was an explosion. She jumped.

"Stand still!" Adam shouted. Something about that spurred her on. She had to do better. She looked at the burned place on the ground and approached it with the tape measure. She set the end down.

"Are you measuring from the center or the edge?" Adam demanded. She hadn't thought of that. She picked the far edge, and got Curtis to hold the tape while she unspooled it to the other end, where she found the far edge of the cone across the yard. She was proud; she'd already learned something.

"Sixty-four!" she called out.

"Sixth-four what?"

"Sixty-four feet." Adam laughed disdainfully. Melanie thought she might die. Her face was hot. She realized her mistake and gave it to him in meters, a shift from which she would never return.

They did the same thing three times, for the three different formulas. All measurements metric. When they were all done, he asked them for the winner. Melanie told him it was the one in the middle. He looked and her, and then at Curtis, and said, "Well, which one was that?" Melanie didn't know.

"The compositions were right there on the cones."

Curtis looked at her. "I thought you were keeping track," he said. Adam looked at them both, and his face started to get red, like he was actually angry, like it was more than a Saturday afternoon play science experiment they'd ruined.

"Never," he said, "never, never assume somebody else has an accurate record of something you're doing if you haven't seen it with your own eyes." Melanie felt like she might cry. It was her fault; she had ruined the experiment.

"I'll fix this," she said. "I'll make up for it."

"Me, too," Curtis said. "What can we do?"

The Brookses had a big two-car garage with an old blue door, and Adam wanted it painted. It was getting on in the afternoon, almost four, the hottest part of the day, and it was probably over a hundred degrees. But he pointed them toward the paint brushes and told Melanie she could go home when they'd finished it, but not a minute sooner. They'd have to sand it first and it was probably going to take two coats but he didn't care. He wanted them to remember this. Not that she would've forgotten it easily. She was terribly ashamed; that's not easy to forget.

When she finally got home, it was dinner time, and she was happy. Someone had finally told her what she was doing wrong. Her parents were sitting side by side on the couch, watching an old movie on TV. They did that often on summer evenings, sometimes even having bowls of ice cream instead of dinner. They told her they'd saved her spot for her, right between them. Her father had this notepad in his lap, and he'd written down some notes about what had happened in the movie so that Melanie could catch up. But she didn't want to sit. She was too keyed up. She wanted to keep going over and over in her mind all the things she had learned that afternoon. She wanted to find every place she'd ever written down something in inches and convert it to centimeters. It felt like more than she'd learned in the whole previous year and she just wanted to keep going.

As she started to explain it to them, what she'd been doing all afternoon, they grew upset.

"You've gotten such a terrible sunburn," her mother said.

"We were worried about where you'd gone" said her father. She feared they would call Adam to complain, although of course they were just as afraid of him as Melanie was. She tried to explain it to them, but they just shook their heads.

Her mother said, "That can't possibly have been worth it."

As she told the story, Melanie realized she had never really thought about her mother's words before.

"Worth what?" John asked. "The sunburn? It seems like it was worth a lot."

"No," Melanie said, only then understanding as the words formed in her mouth, "they didn't mean the sunburn. I asked them if I could have my bowl of ice cream, and my father said that you could only ever really be in one place at one time."

She understood, then, what he had meant, and why he'd said it, though she didn't like it.

"I guess their feelings were hurt," John said. "They were thinking about themselves, not about the great things you were going on to do in your life." She remembered the hum of the freezer, her parents' faces in the flicker of the television. She thought of Dean, going back into the crowded restaurant alone.

"So did he give it to you?" John asked. "The ice cream?"

Melanie looked down at her leg in its cast. She couldn't feel it, couldn't feel her elbow or her shoulder or her ribs. "Yes," she said, "and it was my favorite, mint chocolate chip." She knew then that she would never have the place she wanted in her work, unless she was willing to go there utterly alone.

"Well," John said. "Your parents were terribly kind."

"They're my parents," she said. "They had to be."

"Are they still alive?"

"Yes," she said. "They're still there, in that same house, in the desert. I haven't been there in, gosh, seven years?" She hadn't realized until she said this how unforgivably long it had been. And yet she felt sure that if she returned, they would forgive her.

Footsteps approached in the hall, and she thought it must be Dean, that she could explain what she now understood, that she could apologize and he would come back to her, that his proclamation, *that's it*, would be rescinded and she would have another chance, but the footsteps continued without slowing, down the hall, past her room, on to see somebody else.

ADAM BROOKS, 1961

ADAM ISN'T SURE WHOSE idea it was that his crew should travel to Nevada to watch a test. Probably Stan's; Stan is, at least nominally, in charge of his little unit, the link between Adam and the head of the T division. Stan had said that Adam should be ready at ten on Wednesday morning, and if any of his guys wanted to go, they should be ready then, too. He has two guys. They both want to go.

Stan hasn't meddled much with Adam's team; he largely leaves them alone to calculate things and to dream up new things to calculate. And he isn't meddling now; they weren't given any tasks in connection with this test. In fact, it isn't even a Los Alamos device being exploded, but rather, one from Teller's lab in California. But Adam likes Stan. He drops by Adam's tiny, immaculate office from time to time to check in. Every now and then, the two of them go to dinner. They talk mostly about science, a little bit about their wives, and once about where they might go next. Stan thinks he might like to move back to a university before too long, but he thinks Adam has a plum position and should stay put as long as possible. Where else would he have a mandate for basic research (most everyone else was pressed into service for bomb building), a team of incredibly bright guys to work with, a group of a hundred of the world's greatest physicists within throwing distance, and no teaching or writing obligations? He had already had a good deal of success, in his four years there, and Stan thought he would only rise higher.

When Adam arrives in the lounge area near Stan's office at

five minutes to ten, Larry, and Sol—his guys—are already there. He wonders if the two of them came over together, if they met up without him. Not that he would've gone if they had invited him; he spent the early morning having a long breakfast with his wife. The day still feels momentous. Perhaps it's the two flights he'll take, one on a small plane that will take them low under the clouds to Albuquerque, and one on a commercial jet to Las Vegas. Or maybe it's the sheer fact that he will finally get to see an atomic bomb explode, after more than a decade of thinking about them, calculating their possibilities, feeding numbers, through circuitous paths, into them. He wonders if this is how movie directors feel when they get into the limousines that ferry them to their premieres.

Larry has been to a test before, a few years earlier in the Pacific. Adam had been scheduled to go but his son had been born a week before so they'd sent Larry instead. Now he is talking about it. "We sat around a lot," he says. "I mean, we got there way in advance, and there wasn't a lot to do." Now he has books with him. Novels, Adam sees. He wonders if he should've brought something to read, some journals to catch up on, transcripts of lectures. But he doesn't want to sit around reading. He wants it all to be happening.

Stan appears at two minutes past ten, and the five of them walk together out into the hot late morning.

"It'll only be hotter up there," says Larry. "That thing might detonate itself." Sol doesn't say anything. He is Adam's favorite of the three, a Cal Tech man like himself, married, though not yet with any children. He had been two years ahead of Adam at Cal Tech as an undergraduate, then gone to Korea with the army. Once when a water main had burst and none of the taps were working anywhere in the tech area, Sol had disappeared, and returned a few minutes later with a five-gallon jug of distilled water from the supply room, which he used to make their group a pot of strong coffee. All morning people were popping into their area asking if they had any left.

When they deplane at McCarran, there is a government car

waiting for them, surely, Adam thinks, because Stan is with them. His little group doesn't merit this level of service. He checks his watch; it's still barely four pm and the test isn't until the next day.

"Good thing I brought these," Larry says, slapping the side of his bag with the books in it.

"Don't think you'll be needing those," says Stan from the front seat. "We've got a better way to kill some time around here."

"What's that?" Adam asks.

"You ever play blackjack?" Stan asks.

"What, cards?" says Sol.

"I've never played," Adam says. His mental picture of casinos comes from the movies, and even this is hazy; he has been to the movies all of twice since moving to Los Alamos. He had never thought of glitzy, boozy Las Vegas as a real place.

"It's quite simple," Stan says. He explains the rules. Adam listens intently, repeating each step in his mind as Stan talks.

"All right," he says when Stan has finished. "We should be able to beat this thing no problem."

"Famous last words," says Larry. Sol still hasn't said anything. Adam leans over Larry to look at him. He is staring out the window.

"You okay, Sol?" Adam says.

"Fine," Sol says. "I'm not a card player."

"Slots, then," Stan says. "Think you can manage the slots?"

"Sure," Sol says. "I'll play a few. But nobody tell Lisa."

"Oh, mercy," says Stan.

"Let him be," says Adam. He is in too good a mood to let any of this get to him.

"Aw, come on," says Larry when the car stops in front of a one-story white building. There's a massive sign on the roof: El Cortez Hotel. A second sign, the letters stacked vertically on top of one another, says "Gambling." "We're playing here? What about the Sands? What about Harrah's?"

"This is the place for us," says Stan. "They get a call from Mercury on the night before a test to let us all know it's on for the morning. There are these blue lights in the ceiling that come on to tell us the conditions are okay, the test is going forward."

"No shit?" Larry says. "Inside the casino?"

"Would I lie to you?" Stan says.

Adam looks around. It is kind of shabby, a third-rate establishment at best, but he doesn't care. He doesn't need glitter and bright lights.

The four of them walk into the casino in a straight line, Stan at the front, Sol at the back. The air is smoky, so much so that it's difficult to see very far into the room. Larry disappears toward the poker tables. Sol stands like a lost child until Stan puts a hand on his shoulder and points him toward the slots. "You guys do this every time?" Adam asks Stan when they are alone.

"Not much else to do around here," Stan says. "Mercury isn't exactly a hotbed of social activity. I keep thinking one of these days we could play out a few thousand games on MANIAC. Get the perfect formula to beat the house." MANIAC is the supercomputer they use to run out calculations for the bombs.

"I'll bet we do pretty well just running the numbers up here." Adam taps his temple. "How many decks are they using?"

"Six or seven, I'd say." Stan steers him toward a table. It's dirty and smoky. He and Stan buy in for twenty dollars apiece. To his right, he can see Sol, walking up and down a row of slot machines, squinting at them.

At first he has a little trouble keeping up with the pace of the game, remembering the rules for how the dealer will play his hand, but soon he is settled in. Each hand presents a simple question of statistics, and the entire game is a closed system for which he can account. After a couple of hours, Larry rounds them all up and they eat a cheap, greasy dinner. Adam and Larry each drink a beer; Sol declines, and Stan, who orders last, declines as well. Adam thinks maybe he should've passed, too.

They hang around their table for a while. Adam starts sketching out the program they might run on MANIAC on the back of a napkin. He passes it to Larry. Larry copies it over onto his own napkin, with a few changes, and passes it back. Adam tucks both napkins into his shirt pocket. He probably won't actually run the program; there will be more pressing matters when they get back to the lab. Still, he likes the idea. He likes the possibility of it, the fact that this entire city is full of people playing games that could be perfected by a big box of wires.

Around nine they head back onto the floor and play some more. Adam has already won a little over two hundred dollars, and moves to a table with a higher limit. He wouldn't have thought he'd enjoy this, but in the end, it's just a math problem, and he has fun with the little tweaks he can make to his play. He joins Larry at the poker tables for a while, has another beer, then more blackjack. He thinks about what he might do with the cash. He could change some of it to silver or gold coin and keep it, in case all this weapons business gets out of hand; if the world dissolves in some kind of nuclear chaos, he can't count on currency. And beyond that, he thinks he'd like to find a nice gift for Angeline. They'll have a fifth anniversary next year, and he hasn't given her much of anything since the tiny engagement ring he'd scraped together from his graduate student's stipend.

"What would you get your wife?" he asks Stan, who has quit playing and settled at the bar. He shows him his handful of chips.

"Well, God damn," Stan says. "You sure you haven't been here before?"

He gives Stan a weak smile. "I think I'd like to get her something. A surprise, you know? I just don't really know what she'd want."

"No man ever went wrong with diamonds," Stan says. "We could stop somewhere on our way through on Friday. Maybe a bracelet. Nancy's always admiring those on other people. What do you call 'em, you know, a tennis bracelet."

"You going to get her one?"

"I haven't been as lucky out there as you," Stan says.

"Maybe you just need to play bigger," Adam says. They sit a while longer, Stan slowly drinking a beer. Larry is nowhere to be seen, and Sol is back by the slots again.

Without warning, Stan jumps up from his stool. "It's on," he says. He points to a blue lightbulb over the door that has come on. It's almost two. "Cash out," he says. "I'll get the others, and we'll hit the road."

The car is out in front of the casino. Whether it's been there the whole time, waiting, or has returned, Adam doesn't know. Soon all four of them are in it, speeding North. Nobody says anything. Adam likes the silence, but he can tell it's bothering Sol, who keeps breathing in like he's going to say something, then letting his breath out again in silence. Out the window it's pitch black, though even if it were light, Adam thinks, there would be nothing to see. They're barely out of the riotous light and noise of Las Vegas, but this is nothingness.

In about an hour, they arrive at a gate, where the driver rolls down his window; they are waved inside. The car stops outside a cluster of temporary-looking buildings. "We've got about two hours," Stan says. "Get some rest." He leads them into one of the buildings. There are bunks. Adam climbs onto one and stretches out on top of the blanket. It's cold—difficult to believe, given the heat of the day, but then, this is the desert. He barely has time to straighten himself out, witness the slight turning out of his right leg as he relaxes into the thin mattress, before he is asleep.

A voice comes over the loudspeaker. "H minus one minute." He slides the dark glasses on, dimly aware of Stan beside him, doing the same. Thirty seconds later, another warning. The first test they did of the Super, in the Pacific a couple of years ago, went off a few seconds early. Adam knows this, though he was still in school at the time, the men doing the building and testing still just names.

When the ten-second warning sounds, he turns his back, though he keeps his shaded eyes open. His mind is blank.

There is no sound. Everything goes bright and silent. Brighter than daylight. Then, there is a painful click in his ears, not a sound, but a physical impact. The shock wave, he thinks, though it is difficult to connect this new sensation with the familiar term. He gives his head a hard shake. It feels as though a tiny insect with pointed hooks has crawled into his ear, and is boring a hole in his eardrum.

Then comes the sound, a big rolling boom. He turns around to see the fireball. It is enormous, covering the whole horizon. The fire is on fire. He is on fire.

He stares and stares through the glasses. He wants to take them off, but he doesn't dare. This is not what he has seen in photographs of previous explosions. This is not what he has heard described, not what Larry saw the last time, not what Adam has calculated in his ever-growing series of equations describing the possibilities for the release of energy from uranium isotopes.

Later, he will learn that this was the largest explosion ever set off, forty-four kilotons. But now, here, what he sees is the sky, the air turning impossibly bright and dark at the same time, then all that brightness, all the brightness in the world, being sucked into that cloud as it spreads over the desert just before dawn.

He clinks two silver dollars together in his pocket. He could have held one up, right in front of his eye, measuring the size of the blast as he knows observers before him have done, but it wouldn't have blocked this out. His mind is still empty, all the numbers that could describe this now out of his reach. It still feels bright and silent. He can feel Stan beside him, looking at him, waiting to share a reaction, but he can't turn.

DEFENSE

IT'S ONLY ABOUT AN hour's drive to Santa Fe. Charlotte Katz notes the odometer reading in her log. The morning air is cool, the roads clear, and she is in the parking lot at the train station—the designated meeting place—at quarter to eleven. These are the sorts of days she likes best in her work, freed from the desk and screen, out on the road. She sits in her car and quiets her anxiety as best she can by reminding herself what she is doing. She had fallen asleep thinking of her client, Diego Salerno, and awakened with thoughts of his wife, who is also his co-defendant. He has been accused of trying to sell restricted information on America's nuclear program to a foreign nation. A twenty-two count indictment names him and his wife in a conspiracy. But after seeing all the documents and hearing his story, Charlotte is inclined to believe that his motives were neither financial nor political. He had a theory for how to create nuclear energy more efficiently, and no one at Los Alamos was interested in implementing it, and more than anything, he just wanted to see it built, somewhere, anywhere. She wants desperately to get the evidence to make her case. If she can prove that he did not have information that was truly vital, they might stand a chance. And maybe, just maybe, this witness can do it.

When she enters the station, Dr. Brooks marches right up to her, sticks out a hand and introduces himself. He wears a checked flannel shirt tucked into faded jeans. His hair is white and in need of a trim. He is clean-shaven. He looks just how she imagined a great scientist would look. "Let's go," he says. "You can buy me a cup of coffee." Without waiting for a reply, he starts for the door. She gathers her things and follows him, catching up just as they reach the street.

"I appreciate your taking the time," she says. He turns right. Ahead is a café with a brightly painted sign that reads "Good Coffee."

"I don't have science training," she says. "But I understand that Dr. Salerno was involved more in the generation of energy than in weapons design, and that he had a particular method that he felt—"

"Hydrogen flouride lasers," Adam Brooks says. They reach the café and he holds the door open for her. It's a small space, six tables, five of them empty, the last occupied by a middle-aged man in jeans, engrossed in a newspaper.

"What would you like?" Charlotte asks. "Do you want something to eat?"

"Coffee. Cream and sugar." He takes a seat at a table in the back.

There are names she has heard before. Oppenheimer, obviously. Feynman. Bradbury. Brooks is not one of them. She googled him, when she'd finally managed to convince Diego to give her a list of people she could talk to. His name was out there; he had certainly been an important figure at the lab, not during the war, but right when Diego was there, in the 60's and 70's. He had made the bombs bigger, and later, he had worked on the nonproliferation treaty, always behind the scenes. She has a good feeling about him as a witness. She brings the two cups and takes her place across from him.

"So," he says, not waiting even for her to get her notepad ready. "Salerno has finally gotten himself into trouble. I guess we all end up somewhere."

"I'm hoping there's no 'ending up' involved in this," she says. Something about his demeanor, his brazen grab of authority, has made her own tone sharper, more certain. She clicks open her retractable pen with more force than is necessary.

"You have to wonder if this is what he wanted. He had choices, that man. Still has his health. Still has his wife." She senses a judgment in Adam Brooks's tone, a superiority. *No*, she wants to say. *It's not what he wanted.*

"How did you know about the charges?" she asks.

"It was in the paper." He takes a sip of coffee. There is a bitterness in his expression, a slight downturn of the mouth, eyes cast to the side.

"I'm hoping you can tell me a little bit about what kind of person he was. What kind of scientist, what kind of employee."

"I didn't know he was doing this, if that's what you're after. Arranging this sale, or transfer, or however it ended up."

"That's not what I'm asking." He doesn't seem frightened, like a witness who fears he, too, will be accused, but he is ill at ease. "I'm more interested in how he worked, in what kind of guy he was, in what kinds of things motivated him. Did he work for you?"

"Not directly."

"But you had some say in his supervision?"

"I had some say in most things. Including hiring Diego. And firing him." He dips his little finger in the coffee, then puts it in his mouth. Something in his tone tells her that despite what google has told her—that he was not among the very top leadership, not in the most exclusive meetings—that it is very important to him that she believe this. He looks back toward her, though he keeps his eyes focused slightly above hers. "I always thought it may have been a mistake," he says, more softly than she has yet heard him speak. She leans down, trying to catch his gaze from below.

"Which? Hiring or firing?"

"Both, I suppose."

"Say more."

"Well, now, I don't know. You aren't going to try to bring me down there to testify or anything like that, are you?"

"It depends on what you have to say."

"I won't get on a stand and say all this to a room full of

reporters. I'm too old to have some self-righteous journalist going back through all the decisions I made and picking them apart with the benefit of hindsight. If someone wants to do that they'll have to wait until I'm dead." His voice is rising steadily.

"Let's not worry about testimony right now," she says. "I'm just trying to put together my strategy and if you can help me understand him, understand what was true and what was possible." She waits for a reply, but he just grunts, a sound so noncommittal that it might have been nothing more than an unhappy exhale. He looks down at the table. Then, he begins to speak.

"Diego's idea involved an entirely different kind of laser from what we were using."

"You mentioned hydrogen flouride."

"So you were paying attention. He thought it was cheaper and more effective than the system we had."

"And?"

"It was." She feels these words in her fingertips, an almost-pain like static electricity. She can see Dr. Salerno's small eyes, the way they bore into her when he talks about his work. In an instant, all has become clear: this was his plan all along. Prison was, if not a part of it, a known possibility he'd been willing to endure. What he had not anticipated was that they would take his wife. Charlotte wonders if the wife really did play a part, or if this is the government's way of building leverage. But she isn't leverage enough; Diego will press on, and it is that fact that seems to torture him. Her pen rests in her hand, useless.

The case is precarious. A week ago, she visited Diego, prepared to do her utmost to win him over to her strategy for the case. She'd been hassled by the guards on the way in, and she was rattled. Diego lifted his head when the guard unlocked the door, and though he didn't smile—he never smiled—she detected a hint of pleasure near the corners of his mouth. She had caught him on a good day.

"How've you been?" she asked, reaching out to shake his hand as the door swung shut behind her.

"It is terrible in here," he said.

"Is it getting worse? Did something happen?"

"Every day it is all the same. These boys here, they are saying the rudest things, and there is nothing to eat."

"I'm still trying to get you transferred," she said. "At least until your trial. But they seem to be concerned that you'll try to leave the country."

"I will not. I promise you I will not if I can just sleep in a bed and eat food that has some, some, what, taste to it. Spice," he said.

"I know you won't. But I'm having trouble convincing the government." She has spent hours on the phone, without much hope.

"Tell me about it," he grumbled. "The government cannot be convinced."

She smiled, hoping that this was a small joke at his own expense. She has two dozen bankers boxes in her office, photocopies of the treatises he has composed over the years and Fed-Exed to people in various government agencies.

"We need to discuss our strategy," she said. Diego squinted at her, as though she were a bird high in a tree. He looked even older than when they last met a week before, his eyes sunken, his skin sagging. "Remember the day when we went through the indictment together and looked at every count and what they all meant?"

"It is all wrong," he said. "I am not trying to hurt this country. It is a good country. But they won't listen." His gray-tinged skin began to flush. She had heard this speech four times already. She wanted to cut him off, to get on with it. She hates it when clients do this, repeat ad nauseam that they've done nothing wrong, refuse to be realistic about their choices, their situations, refuse to believe that she might actually know what's best. Diego was still talking, little droplets of saliva flying from his mouth. "And then they throw me in jail when I try to tell anybody else about it. I don't know what kind of country you people think you are running here where you throw people in jail for having good ideas."

"I know." She took a deep breath and tried to conjure back the words she had practiced, to calm her frustration. She could see the little window in her office, the mirror where she tried to get the worry out of her brow as she rehearsed. "But I can't go in there and tell a jury that you didn't send information to this Luis person, this agent. They've got the documents you sent him. They've got photos of you meeting him. You had plane tickets. I don't know how you think I'm going to explain away two tickets to Venezuela."

"How can they say I gave it to Venezuela when the only person I ever talked to was not actually from Venezuela?"

"We've been through this," she said. "They just have to show that you meant to." This part, in particular, frustrates her. Diego is too smart to have honestly believed that the phone calls he was making would get him transferred to real-life high level officials in the Venezuelan government, their nuclear program. The agent who had been corresponding with him had testified about how easy it was to fool him, as though there were some extra professional pride attached to duping a man with a Ph.D.

"I'm not a traitor. They're the traitors. The government people make me do this and then they throw me in prison for doing it. You know this." It was all she could do to keep from rolling her eyes. She has more contempt for Diego Salerno than she ever has for her more run-of-the-mill clients, men who lost their tempers, drunk drivers, addicts. Diego Salerno is privileged, and intelligent, and could easily have prevented all this. He is fully capable of understanding what is happening, what needs to be done, and still, he fights her.

"That's not going to get you anywhere," she said. He slumped in his chair. He was listening, but she could tell that he didn't like listening to her, thirty-two years old, five foot three. She rifled through her file and slid out the indictment. "Remember this? How we talked about each of these individual charges, and the pieces they have to prove for each one?"

"It had my name on it forty-seven times. In that dark print. And Carol's name thirty-three times. I don't see why they had to get Carol. I don't see why they can't let me explain and send her home."

"They might do just that," Charlotte said. Diego's face softened then, the anger tinged with sadness.

"It isn't right," he said, shaking his head.

"That's beside the point. We need to think in terms of what they can prove." Diego extended his hand and wrapped his thumb and forefinger around Charlotte's forearm. She stiffened; he had never touched her before, except for the handshake at the beginning of each visit. His hands were large, her arms thin. Her eyes tracked involuntarily toward the door. She could see the back of the guard's head through the little window.

"Some things are true even if I can't prove them, Miss Katz," he said. He released her arm.

"We can't very well argue that you didn't make the drops," she said, following her script, her voice higher and faster than she wanted it to be. "They have photos. We can't argue that you didn't take money for information. But they may not be able to prove that you actually had any information that was valuable. If you weren't a true insider, then they can't establish half their case, and even if they got all the rest, you could be looking at as little as—"

"I knew everything that went on in that lab," he said. He sat up straighter in his chair. She had expected anger at the suggestion, a roar of animal rage. Instead, his voice was barely audible. "I knew every last secret about the laser program, and if you gave me a lab and a modest budget, I could get you a small nuclear arsenal in two years just out of what's in here." He gave his left temple two slow taps with a broad finger.

"Look," she said. "I know you think you didn't do anything wrong. But I've got this figured out. It's the best way to try to knock out some of those charges and keep you out of prison. It's the only part of this with any give."

"You want to tell them I was…" He paused, searching for the

word. "Expendable." He locked her eyes. She felt a trickle of sweat begin in the middle of her spine and drip toward her waistline. "Yes?"

"It's not that *I* think you were expendable." Her heart was racing. "But we're just going to have to tell the twelve people on your jury that you didn't know quite as much as you have suggested you did. Maybe if we can get some other people from the lab who might be willing to say that you might have tried to make it seem like you—"

"Make it seem like what, Miss Katz?" The taste of blood filled her mouth. She had bitten the inside of her cheek. "Like I was just some vain, self-important fool?" Her throat stung with acid. She was in fourth grade again, caught outside the fence during recess, made not just to serve her punishment, but to personally call her father at work from the principal's office while three teachers stood over her, listening. She swallowed.

"Look," she said. "This is about keeping you out of prison."

"I'd rather stay in prison."

"No, you wouldn't. If the jury thought you were a fool rather than a traitor, then they might—"

"Get out," he said.

"You have to listen."

"I said get out." She looked at the door, at the blue jumpsuit.

"I'm the only attorney they're going to give you," she said. "I'm trying to keep you out of prison, not win you a Nobel Prize." He crossed his arms and stared into the far corner of the room, as if there were some insect crawling there in the corner, digging itself into the wall. His chest expanded slowly and shrank again. It rose and fell four times, five, six, seven.

Dr. Brooks continues. "He was there less than a year when he started harping on it. Every meeting, and in between, he'd be at my door, he'd be at everyone's door with some new calculation. Son of a bitch would not give up."

She wants to pause the conversation for a moment, to catch up, but he is barreling along. She clicks the pen open again and tries to start writing, but no ink comes out. He's speaking fast, as though he'd had all this saved up and couldn't keep all the words in his mouth any longer. "We had to make choices so we could move forward. You're too young to remember, but it was a race. If we divided our resources in building three different cars, no one of them could win."

"You're right," she says, "I don't remember. I've only read about it." She is beginning to shape, in her mind, the story she now understands Diego would like her to tell. She realizes she had been operating on the assumption that he was wrong about the lasers, that if his idea had been so brilliant, it would have been implemented.

"Would you say that he was selfish? That he wanted it his way because it was his way?"

"No," Dr. Brooks says quickly. Then, he is quiet for a long time. Charlotte resists the temptation to ask a further question. "I didn't know the man that well. I only knew his work. But if I had to say, I'd guess that he honestly believed it to be best."

"Has that ever happened to you? You knew for sure, and nobody would listen?"

"Oh, we listened. We just decided against it. Rightly or wrongly."

"Let me rephrase that. Have you ever had an idea you were sure would work that was decided against?"

"I made the decisions." She drains her coffee cup. She sees now how this man can help. He will be a key piece of the puzzle, the credibility they need.

Charlotte went back to the prison four days after Diego threw her out. They were busy days; she had had a court appearance in another case that went poorly, and a women's bar association luncheon, and a long-ago promised dinner at the law school. Her emotions around Diego had cooled some. Staying late in the office, to the sound of vacuum cleaners, she felt she had gotten it under control.

She had written it all down, an individual page for each potential strategy, sketching out the arguments she would make, the kinds of evidence that would be involved. She had given each one a number, her estimation of its chances of success. If Diego wouldn't talk with her, at least she could leave the papers behind, and he would eventually understand that she was right about this. She had never known a man in prison to refuse to read something, if she waited long enough. He would study them, and sooner or later, he would see that she was right.

"So you are back," he said. He was standing this time, his back straight, the legs of his jumpsuit too short, exposing his white, hairless ankles.

"You need something from me, and I need something from you," she said. "We don't need to have a long visit if you'd rather not."

"Are you going to insult me again?" He took a wide stance, as though preparing to resist a blow.

"No," she said. "Nor did I insult you last time."

He grunted.

She reached up to adjust her collar. "This is all a matter of strategy. It's a game we can win, like chess. Do you play chess?"

"This is not chess," he said. "I am sitting all day and all night in a filthy prison while people out there call me names, and you want me to pretend I'm some kind of nobody just to get back out into a world where everyone will think I'm an imbecile."

"All right," she said, her exasperation building. "It's not chess. But we can still out-smart them and win with the right strategy. It's about taking those charges in the indictment and poking little holes in them, one by one by one, until they forget any of the individual things we might have said about you in the process, because you're a free man. *They're* the ones who are going to look foolish. You have to trust me. I know what I'm doing."

He pulled his plastic chair out from behind the table and sat heavily, resting his elbows on his knees. "Yes, they are very foolish. Can't see what's sitting there right on their noses."

"All right, then. We agree." She took her chair. "I'm going to show you four strategies." She opened her portfolio.

"Wait," he said.

She looked up, marking her place in the papers with one finger.

"You said you wanted something from me."

"Yes," she said. "I'm going to need some names."

"You sound just like the government men."

"No, not those kinds of names. I want to know who in the lab really knew you. Who understood what you were doing, and why."

"Nobody understood. They fired me."

She sighed. "Look, I can't help you if you don't cooperate with me. There must have been some people, along the way somewhere, who saw what you were trying to do. I'm not going to get anyone in trouble. I just want to hear what they might have to say. What kind of witnesses they might be."

He peered at her, still suspicious. "How do I know I can trust you?"

"I'm your attorney," she said. "I'm duty-bound to act in your best interests."

"Duty," he said. He fixed her with his stare. "You think that means anything? I have a duty. I was trying to fulfill it and it landed me here."

"You know, when I take court appointments like this, they pay me about a quarter of what I usually get paid, and then I come in here and you yell at me. Why would I bother if I didn't care about getting you off?"

"I want you to do something for me," he said. "To prove it."

"What's that?"

"Take a note to my wife," he said.

"You know I can't do that. You're charged with conspiracy. It's strictly forbidden for you to—"

"What, tell a frightened old woman who was only trying to help her husband that he loves her?"

"It's obstruction of justice," she said. "You and I could both be charged, and nothing we've said here today would be privileged anymore, and I could lose my license."

"And wouldn't that be a shame."

This sarcasm stung. She thought quickly. She needed the names to build her case. It was out of the question that she deliver a note. It would be too easy to trace, and the stakes were too high. But even if she did take a note, the wife could not send a reply; how would he ever know, until after the trial, whether it had gotten there or not? It would be a lie, a bald lie, but not at anyone's expense.

"I'll do it," she said. She tore two sheets from her legal pad and passed him her pen. "Three names on this sheet, contact information if you know it, the note on this one. But I get to read it. If it says anything about the case, deal's off." He gave a barely detectable nod.

"Show me your files," he said. "What you brought. The strategy."

She lay the four sheets out on the desk, facing him. She had buried her preferred route in the middle, but it didn't fool him. His hand went right to it, and he pushed it away; he did not wish her to prove that the reports he sold were old news, his so-called secrets relatively commonplace principles of physics, his claims of inside knowledge inflated. He also quickly rejected the one on the far left, the attempt at a plea bargain that she thought the U.S. Attorney was unlikely to accept even if she could convince Diego to talk. The two that remained were what she thought of, as she prepared them, as the suicide missions: a flat denial in the face of a mountain of evidence, or the cold truth, that the science is correct, that the U.S. has been mismanaging the program, that Diego Salerno was no spy, no traitor, but a whistleblower bravely insisting on a different path, one that needed to be explored, if not by the United States, then by someone else. A media circus of a trial, sure to end in a swift verdict and a severe sentence. The denial, she thought, stood a chance; she didn't yet know just how much evidence there really was, if any of it was vulnerable, if a skillful cross-examination might weaken it enough to pry a juror or two loose.

"I'm going to leave all four of these here," she said. "You can read them in more detail and think them over, and I can continue to gather information."

He did not respond. He was staring at the first sheet from her legal pad, whether trying to summon the names of those who were once his allies, or considering what he might say to his wife, she could not tell. She looked away, trying to give him some sense of privacy; this time alone with her was all the solitude he got.

Once he began to write, he did not pause; he wrote the note first, four short lines, and then switched smoothly to the second sheet, where he wrote three names, two of them with addresses.

"We'll meet in a couple of days," she said. "We'll figure this out."

He passed her the two sheets.

"She was never supposed to be a part of this," he said.

You did nothing wrong, the note read. *I am safe, and I hope you are. I am sorry this happened to us. I love you.* It was neither addressed nor signed. She slipped it into her file with the list of names. As she stood to leave, Diego Salerno offered his hand, and she took it, and for the first time she noticed how frail it was, how cold.

When she got home, Charlotte retreated to her tiny home office, with its pale pink walls, the room the previous occupants had used as a nursery. Her desk filled one entire wall, the small window to her left, the door behind her when she sat, the wall to her right full of floor-to-ceiling bookshelves of law school books, spare copies of the rulebooks, a collection of popular books about lawyers that people had given her over the years. She hooked up her laptop and kicked off her heels. She could've change into jeans, poured a glass of wine, put something on the stereo, but she didn't feel as though she was really home yet. The room was an island, halfway between her downtown office and her bedroom, its walls so close that when she spread her arms, she could touch both at the same time, depending on how long she had allowed her fingernails to grow.

She liked the tightness of the space. Sometimes the rest of the house felt too big, too empty, although it was only 1,200 square feet. It had been six months since her last girlfriend, Leah, moved out, over a year since her mother had come to visit, and all the space served only to remind her of this. Leah had been a schoolteacher, had filled surfaces with ungraded papers and handouts and ideas. She had a loud laugh. Charlotte's mother was the sort of person who quietly talked to herself, asking little questions that weren't meant to be answered, always letting you know she was nearby, going about her day.

Charlotte set the note and list of names in the center of her desk. She read the note over, then read it again. *I'm sorry this happened to us.* Yes, she thought, he is genuinely sorry, if not for any of the rest of it, for what this has done to his wife. It was the first glimmer of vulnerability she saw from him. She felt something shift in her, found herself wildly wanting, in that moment, not just to minimize his sentence, but to help him. It was not the professional desire she always had with her clients, the duty, the drive to win. It was something broader, that followed her here, into her quiet home. She had before her a man who loved his wife, who, without meaning to, had put her in harm's way, who wanted desperately to change that. She felt that fact like longing, like loss.

She picked up the list. The first name, Jim Garrison, had an address in Pasadena. The second, Ed MacMillan, was in Washington. She'd never heard either name, and couldn't tell from the addresses if they were offices or condos. The third name was by itself, no address, no phone number, not even a city, but it had a little star beside it. Adam Brooks.

A search turned up hundreds of people named Adam Brooks. She tried "Adam Brooks Science," but that did little to help. "Adam Brooks Physics" was better, and "Adam Brooks Nuclear" yielded four phone numbers. She glanced at the clock. 6:15. These were most likely office numbers, where no one would answer at this hour, but she couldn't take her eyes from the note, lying there on her desk, its pain seeping into her, spurring her to action.

The first number rang seven times before she hung up. The second was answered immediately.

"Yes?" a woman said.

"Good evening." She realized that she'd dialed a number in New York; it was 8:15. "I'm sorry to disturb you. Is there a Mr. Brooks there?" There was a silence. "Hello?" she said.

"Who's calling?"

"I'm an attorney representing an old colleague of his. I was just hoping to talk for a few minutes."

"Hold on." The woman had apparently set the phone down; Charlotte heard footsteps, then muffled voices, the woman's, and a man's. She could not make out the words, but there was a tension in the tones. Finally, a man picked up.

"Who is this?"

"Adam Brooks?"

"I'm his grandson."

"Terribly sorry to disturb you," she said. "I'm an attorney, representing a man who once worked with your grandfather. Do you know how I could get in touch with him?" She heard her own voice as though it were someone else's, as though it were a recording.

"I don't know that he'd want to be in touch with any attorney," the man said.

"He's still alive, isn't he?"

"What? Yes, of course, he—"

"I understand if you can't give me his telephone number. Maybe you could just tell me where he lives? What part of the country? What city?"

"I'll tell you what," the grandson said. Charlotte pictured a woman huddled beside him, trying to hear, stroking his hand, the way Leah used to do when she made calls from home in the evenings. "You give me your name and number, and I'll give them to him."

It was still light, and just outside her window, a bird perched in the cottonwood tree. She didn't know what kind of bird it was; she never bothered to learn, not in New York where she went to college, or California at law school, and not here in New Mexico. Her skin began to sting with the day's dried sweat. She always needed a shower when she'd been to a jail.

She stood under lukewarm water, not bothering to soap or shampoo. She thought of Diego, surely made to shower in an open space, watched. She had no hint of the context of his life, just the stained tiles of the visiting room, the dark blue jumpsuit. And he knew nothing of hers, her cluttered office, her empty house. She wondered how she could know a person stripped of context. She wondered if it was already beginning to sink in, that the strategy was a painful one, but the only way to blast down the walls. He could keep his head tipped down in the courtroom, try not to listen, sing some favorite childhood song over and over in his head, never read any reports, hold his breath and wake up, if Charlotte had anything to say about it, a free man.

She shut off the water and reached through the curtain for her towel. It wasn't there. She stood, dripping, before remembering that she'd thrown it in the wash this morning, leaving only the hand towel. She took it. She squeezed the water from her hair, toweled the droplets from her shoulders, her back, her legs, then wrapped the towel around her head. Her cell phone began to ring. She sprinted down the hall, covering herself as best she could as she passed the street-facing window, to her office.

"Charlotte Katz?" The voice was deep, warm. She had only the small towel wrapped around her hair. The office contained nothing of use, not a blanket or a sweater or even a scarf.

"Yes," Charlotte said. "Mr. Brooks?"

"Doctor Brooks. I received a message via my grandson. Something about a colleague."

"Of course, Dr. Brooks, I apologize. I am representing Diego

Salerno in a criminal prosecution stemming from what appears to be a mix-up about some information. He's given me the names of a few people who might be able to shed some light on the situation, just in terms of understanding where he was coming from, and—"

"Oh, don't tell me," Dr. Brooks said. Charlotte could practically hear him rolling his eyes. "Is this to do with the laser?"

"Not directly." She crossed back to the bedroom and began riffling the hangers with her one free hand. "I'm sorry, Dr. Brooks, where are you calling from? Are you still at Los Alamos?"

"I am."

"In that case, might you be willing to meet me in person?"

Diego had surely known what he was doing, giving her this particular name, marking it with a star. She wishes she could call Diego, slip out just for a moment to tell him that she understands now.

"You said you also fired him. Was it because of the lasers?" Dr. Brooks stares at her, silent. He is quiet for so long that she begins to count, to keep herself from speaking. She has made it to twenty-seven before he speaks.

"You are an attorney."

"Yes."

"But I am not your client."

"No."

"Is there a way that I can speak to you in confidence? Not for anybody to hear, not the court, not the lab, not Diego?"

"I can give you my word as a fellow human. It won't be bound by the law, like the attorney-client privilege. But I can promise you."

"And do you?"

"Yes," she says, "I promise."

"There are two people on the planet who know what I'm about to tell you. Myself and my physician." He stiffens in his chair, leans forward as though about to stand, then slumps back. "I haven't got a lot of time left. And there will be a decline. There is a decline."

"You're ill?"

"Yes." Dr. Brooks taps his temple with his right index finger. "I will lose my mind, and then I will lose my body, and then, I will die. Perhaps soon."

"And nobody knows."

"Just myself and my doctor. And you."

"You have a family," Charlotte says. It isn't a question she'd planned; it just comes out. "I spoke to—"

"I have a son. He will know when he knows, and he can tell his family. My wife is gone. There's the lab. They won't need to know. I am no longer relevant."

"Are you in pain?"

"It's not important," Dr. Brooks says.

"I'm sorry to hear that," she says, and she is sorry.

"I don't think Diego is a bad man. Or a bad scientist."

"You can help him. We'll figure out exactly what you need to say."

"I've thought of him, even before he showed up in the news." He lifts his coffee cup, and, finding it cold, puts it down again. "I would probably do the same again. But it never sat quite right." She wants to grab him by the shoulders, to pull him headlong into her defense.

"We'll make it right," she says. "As right as we can. Tell me exactly what happened. You fired him. Were you directly responsible?"

"I was not what you might call the trigger man. But that doesn't mean I was not the architect of that particular decision."

"And it was to do with this? With the laser?"

"In a way." He pauses again. He looks tired, as though this were the end of a long day, not a morning coffee. "It could've been any idea he was obsessed with. He only ever worked on our official projects with half his brain."

"What else might you have done? If you hadn't let him go?"

"I want to tell you—it ought to be known that—" he stops

abruptly. He stares out the window.

"Dr. Brooks? Are you all right? Do you need a glass of water?" Her throat aches, waiting for the next words.

"I am fairly certain now that he was correct. Perhaps I should have taken that route. His route." He closes his eyes and massages his temples. Charlotte's mind is racing, the building blocks of her strategy rearranging themselves as she listens.

"How much better would it be? The laser he wanted?" He doesn't answer. She can see Dr. Salerno's face, his certainty that he'd been doing the right thing, his insistence aimed at everyone in his path, colleagues, superiors, the FBI, and now, at her. "Are we talking about a significant waste of resources?"

"It's possible." He pauses. "Would that keep him out of prison?"

"No," Charlotte says. "I can't see how it could. The law will punish him for what he did, not for why. But I think it would mean a great deal to him to hear you say it."

"Have you seen the bombs?"

"I've seen photographs."

"I have stood two miles away and watched. I have seen four of them." He pauses. She can't tell if this is a yes or a no. "Keep me apprised of this, if you would. I don't want to see that man go to prison."

"I will." She draws a breath, to ask him directly if he will help them, but she doesn't get the chance.

"I cannot testify to all of this," he says. Her stomach seizes.

"You mean you won't."

"It doesn't matter. These things take years. I won't live that long."

"We could do a sworn statement. Recorded testimony."

"I might be able to say that hydrogen flouride lasers are a viable alternative to the system we embraced. Maybe even that they have some possible advantages."

"Can't you say more? What you just told me? That he was right? That you still think so?"

"I have been at this lab for fifty-six years." He clears his throat. He looks toward the ceiling, letting his eyes rest there a moment. "There is a certain understanding of my tenure there."

"Did you know they indicted his wife, too?"

"I did not know that." His tone is flat; his face gives away nothing.

"As far as I can tell, she had nothing to do with it. Diego is so upset about that." She is desperate now, thinking this, if nothing else, might get through to him, as it did to her.

"I don't blame him."

"You can help him," she says. "Both of them. We can help them."

Adam Brooks says nothing. Charlotte looks down at her hands, her unpainted fingernails, at his hands, his wedding ring, the hair on the backs of his fingers, the veins. A woman with a baby strapped to her chest in a sling comes into the café and stands at the counter. Still, Adam says nothing, and in that moment she sees them both, Adam and herself, for what they have always been: people who need to be right more than anything, more than air, more than love.

"All right then," she finally says. She snaps her folder shut, her notepad still blank. She shifts everything to her left hand, preparing for a handshake. But when the moment comes, when he stands, she finds she cannot extend her hand. She sees, in Adam Brooks, what she has been doing wrong all her life. She sees that he knows it too. She sees that he is almost out of time, and has, unforgivably, given up.

She crosses back to the parking lot, the midday sun baking her shoulders and the part in her hair, barely able to think through her anger.

She gets in the car and turns on the radio. The air conditioning is weak, and almost immediately sweat begins to soak into her crisp shirt. She takes off her suit jacket and leans back against the fabric seat of her car. It seems impossible that she might drive back to her office, where her assistant will be neatly feeding documents through a scanner and making sure there are two spaces after every period, or worse, to her home, where her morning coffee cup will still be in the sink, with no one to disturb her peace. She feels it as a personal betrayal. It is no longer just a case, a recalcitrant witness. She needs him.

Adam Brooks comes out of the coffee shop and gets into an old Pontiac. He backs carefully out of his parking space. He turns right, then left at a stop sign, and he is gone. From the sound of it, he will have no one to tell about their meeting, no one to hear whatever version he might come up with to explain himself. Surely he is constructing it in his head, for his own benefit, even now. She has done it herself thousands of times. She has perfected the argument in her own defense, whatever she has done, and even now that she is alone, that has been the quiet end of her every day. But she would never do it—would she?—knowing it was wrong.

It will be a long drive back, and there is much to do for Diego, but for a few more minutes, she sits under the desert sun, unable to put the car in gear. There is no conversation to have, no comment from a companion, or even from a stranger, to crystallize what has gone on. There is no one to see the map as she sees it, a sharp turn in the road. Even Diego will not see it; he is a point on the same map. It is this old building with its wooden siding and its swinging sign, the hot sun and the dust that witnessed it, and she is not ready to leave it just yet.

ADAM BROOKS, 1995

SHE IS MUCH MORE beautiful in person than he imagined she'd be. He isn't sorry for thinking it, not even when he thinks of Angeline waiting for him in the hotel, because it is so obviously true. Of course she was always gorgeous on camera; he had seen her program more than a handful of times. But he had been sure that in person, her skin would be dull, her makeup disgustingly thick, her hair positively immobile. It isn't so.

He did not speak directly to her when the arrangements were made last week. A producer had called. That same producer, a young man in thick plastic glasses, is now showing him where to sit. There had been a brief discussion about whether it would be better to have him in the armchair, facing her like a celebrity guest, or at the desk to her left, like a commentator. It was decided that he should take the desk. It will be a short segment, and the topic is serious. He is not the story; he is the expert, the conduit of information.

He had thought it was strange, at first, when the producer had said it was the treaty they wanted to talk about. He was proud of that part of his work, immensely so, but his involvement had been largely behind the scenes, and wasn't widely known. It would have made much more sense if they'd called him to ask about the bombs themselves, or the underlying science. But they wanted what they wanted, and he knew what he was talking about either way, so he'd agreed. It wasn't the kind of offer most people decline.

The powder brush tickles as it sweeps over his forehead. It is not a sensation he is acquainted with; he has always been a man who simply refused to be tickled. Even his son, after one attempt at the age of four, had understood that he was immune to that sort of thing. But now, this brush in the hand of the makeup girl has ruffled him. The muscles in his cheeks tighten without his directing them to do so. It's all he can do to keep still, to prevent himself from twisting out of the way, from reaching up to swat the brush down. This girl doesn't know him, of course, wouldn't have any reason to see his reaction as a failure of character, as the breaking of a decades-long streak, but he doesn't know who else might be watching.

"It's always the men who squirm," the girl says. "Women are used to it. You're all set." She taps him on the shoulder, almost a little swat, a push, move along.

The first part of the program goes by in a blur. The sort of organized chaos on the set is both familiar and foreign: everyone scrambles before a test, too, but the tone is nothing like this. Oddly, the tone was lighter, he thinks, when they were about to set off a bomb.

On the producer's signal, he slides into his place at the end of the desk. The makeup girl has swooped in and is taking advantage of this break to add powder to the anchor's cheeks. She looks up and smiles at Adam. "Good to meet you," she says, barely above a whisper. She flashes her dazzling smile. He nods. It's warmer under the lights than he had imagined. It reminds him of the Nevada sun. And then everything shifts, and they are on the air.

"Today marks the twenty-fifth anniversary of the Nuclear Non-Proliferation Treaty. The treaty was the result of a monumental diplomatic effort, and was an important step toward making us all feel a little bit safer from the threat of nuclear attack. Joining us to discuss this landmark event is physicist Adam Brooks, who both worked to develop these weapons and was active in the effort to limit their further use. Dr. Brooks, thank you for being with us."

"It's good to be here," he says, cribbing the phrase from thousands of TV guests before him.

"You worked on developing the earliest nuclear weapons, like those we used to put an end to World War II. What motivated you to switch your efforts from development to restriction?"

"Well," Adam says, "I wasn't there for the very first atomic weapons we developed and used." He wonders if he could let the imprecision stand. But no, there will be people watching who will consider it dishonest. "I'm not quite old enough for that. My work has been primarily with the second generation. The hydrogen bomb." She has her face arranged in a tableau of concern, but he detects a slight narrowing of her eyes.

"Right," she says, "of course."

"When the sense of urgency receded a bit, I think we all took a deep breath," Adam says. "I was able to see a bit of the context of what we were doing."

"Tell us, Dr. Brooks, if you can, a little about the process of getting a treaty like this one in place. There's diplomacy at the highest levels, behind closed doors. What is the involvement of someone like you, who comes to the table as a representative of the scientific community?" He watches her red lips as she speaks.

"My role was mainly to communicate what I thought was possible," he says. "What the worst-case scenarios looked like, what peaceful uses there might be for the technology, how fundamentally important it was that we do something to contain this beast that had been unleashed. I couldn't claim to speak for the whole scientific community." Then, impossibly, horrifyingly, she continues.

"But you were the chief liaison between Los Alamos and Washington. When you came to those meetings, what was your approach?"

His bladder feels very full. He wonders where she got her so-called information, if some newsroom intern handed her a set of index cards, or whether she did any of the research herself. It hadn't occurred to him to verify their research skills. It was a major network. She was a famous anchor. He doesn't want them to be angry with him, but he cannot let it stand.

"I didn't have an official role like that," Adam says. "The lab sent leadership. Dr. Bradbury, for instance. I myself have not had the pleasure of meeting the President. The former President."

He sees her blink, surprised, but she doesn't miss a beat. "What can you tell us about the significance of this treaty from a scientific standpoint?" He can smell his own sweat, soaking the underarms of his shirt.

"I believe it's a victory for scientists who see our work as understanding the world around us and improving our quality of life through that understanding," he says. This is the phrase he has been repeating to himself for the last several days. "The lab's weapons served a very important purpose, and our work continues to contribute to our lives in peace. Nuclear energy is the way of the future. Nuclear weapons are not."

"Without treaties like this one, would we still be here today?"

"Who's to say?" Adam says. "But I sleep a little better."

"Dr. Adam Brooks, thank you for joining us."

As soon as the clear signal comes, he is on his feet. "What in the hell was that?" He shouts at the producer.

"You did fine," the producer says. He gives a dismissive wave of his hand. Adam despises him.

"Don't you people do your research? Do you even have any idea who you're interviewing?" He is facing her now.

"We do the best we can with what we have," she says with half a shrug. "Don't blame my staff. This isn't the easiest subject to research."

"I don't want it shown," he said.

"We're live," the producer says. He cocks one eyebrow with such condescension that Adam has to clench his firsts to keep from taking a swing.

"I want it pulled from any rebroadcast. I want it deleted from your archives."

"Lighten up," the producer says. "We've had much worse. Such is television." He looks from her to the producer and back again.

"Sir, you need to get off the set," the producer says. "We've got another segment in about a minute and a half." So that was all; his work done, well or badly, the world was on to the next thing, and none of it was going to matter.

CRAWLSPACE

WHEN I PICTURED THE wake, it was at the old house, though I knew perfectly well that he didn't live there anymore and hadn't for almost thirty years. I knew it would be in some funeral home on the outskirts of Los Alamos, that I would be staying in a Holiday Inn instead of my childhood bedroom, but still, my mental image of the event, from the moment the phone rang, had located it under the dark wooden ceiling of his house on Trinity Drive. He was my father's father, my grandfather, though I'd never called him that, even as a child. He was instead, then and always, Adam Brooks, the great physicist.

Just looking in the window I can tell that everyone in the funeral home has a PhD. I can see it in the awkward fit of their jackets. I could've stayed in New York; what did I want with a room full of people wailing over how brilliant and perfect he had been? But Robin convinced me: weddings, graduations, christenings, and big-ticket birthday parties can be skipped. A funeral can't.

It wasn't the goodbye I was afraid of missing. I wouldn't have minded never seeing him again. But this was the only chance I'd get to see his dead body lying in a casket, to be sure as you can only be when you've seen something with your own eyes. When I walk through the door, I march straight to him and feel a moment of profound, unabashed relief.

Part of me wants to push my way right back out, having gotten what I came for. The room is hot and loud and smells heavily of cheap aftershave. I haven't seen my family in a couple of years, but I don't much want to. They've always followed Adam's lead, and he never valued my talents. "Speed doesn't solve problems," Adam had said when I'd come home with a medal from the high school state championship. "It only makes it easier to run away." My parents murmured their agreement. Even Katie couldn't interrupt Adam when, at Thanksgiving the year I was twenty-four, he launched into an extended criticism of my triumphant first article in the *Times:* those couldn't possibly be the most illuminating quotations available, and who was paying me, anyway, the Democratic party, or a supposedly objective organization?

It wasn't a vendetta against me; even in my worst moments I will give him this much. I was just particularly prone to choices that Adam did not approve of, and particularly unwilling to give them up, so I took most of the beating, and I had no defender. But still, I couldn't stay away. Since the news came, I have been harboring a small, foolish hope: maybe without Adam looming over us all, they will begin to understand me.

When I summon the will to approach my family, standing in a little clump beside a gaudy flower arrangement, Katie bursts into tears and pulls me into a hug, the first I remember since we were children. Her hair is a steely gray now and she's cropped it short. Her bony shoulders dig into my arms as I pat her awkwardly on the back.

"You came," she says. "Oh, Ben, we thought for sure we wouldn't see you."

"Of course I came," I say. Our parents greet me solemnly, tearily. They are too deep in their grief to say much. My father's nose is running, and he seems to have stopped trying to keep up with it. My mother's long gray hair is all in a tangle.

The four of us stand together in the front corner of the room. The periodic approach of visitors alleviates the need for us to talk to one another, and anyway, I would want them to say things I know they won't: *He never was good to you. We're sorry we had to choose. We're sorry we always chose him.*

There are at least fifty people here, mostly scientists. In Los Alamos, even now when the lab has expanded to include other types of science, Adam's contributions to atomic physics are akin to sainthood. Every word I overhear is a kind one: brilliant, unparalleled, groundbreaking. I recognize almost no one, though I do spot Carl Chesterfield, a once-frequent visitor to Adam's old house on Trinity Drive, where he had beckoned to me every time we met and produced a quarter from behind my ear. He smoked a pipe and always smelled of sweet tobacco. I see Mrs. Feeny, my ninth grade math teacher. Two of Katie's friends from high school, recognizable through wrinkles and extra weight, are nibbling on cookies by the buffet. No one else looks familiar.

When the news came, Robin offered to come along. I said no. As much as I don't belong in this family, she is positively repelled by it. In the six years of our marriage, Adam never expressed a desire to meet her. He wouldn't have liked her. She's too intuitive, too willing to accept that for which she has no evidence. We were making love when the call came, and it was she who sensed that I ought to answer.

We've been in an ongoing discussion, Robin and I, over a span of years. She wants children, but the prospect fills me with terror. Such responsibility, so many choices, millions of places to go wrong—I can't bear the thought of ruining a life, permanently warping someone's psychology. *Maybe in a year or two,* I tell her. *I'm just not ready.*

"I'm not getting any younger," Robin says. She's thirty-seven.

"Women are having babies later and later," I say. "Into their forties."

"And I intend to have one," she says. "I'd like it to be with you." I want to give her everything she needs, but every time I try to say yes, I say no. These arguments won't last much longer. The decision is mine to make: find a way to get past it, or let her go.

Carl Chesterfield approaches. I'm glad for the familiar face. Perhaps he will even do his old quarter trick, and I won't feel quite so much like I've stumbled into the wrong funeral. He starts with my father, patting him gently on the back, then kisses my mother on the cheek and clasps Katie's hand. Then he comes to me.

"Who's this fellow?" he says. I wait for one of them to remind him. Carl, that's Ben, they'll say. My son. My brother. The room roars around us. No one speaks.

Finally, I step in and introduce myself.

"Oh, yes, yes," Carl says. "The little boy with the notebooks." He means the journals I kept as a boy, scribbled in mirror-writing in a vain attempt at privacy. "Sorry for your loss," he adds. For the first time since the news came, sadness hits me.

"Thank you very much," I say to Carl Chesterfeld. "Excuse me." I've had enough of this.

There is a small empty room off the main parlor with a handful of chairs and a box of tissues. The room where they take people who become upset. I take a seat. Robin meant well with her advice, but she doesn't understand. I remember the first time I began to see that they would never claim me as their own. I was eight years old, and grumpy. I'd been dragged along to help Adam move to a new home when I would've preferred to stay in my room, putting the finishing touches on my elaborate village of Legos. Though in theory we were coming only to make a few trips with our van full of boxes, my father had insisted we get an early start, and had blocked out an extra day in our schedules to allow for the sorting and packing he knew we'd have to do.

We pulled up shortly after nine. My father knocked, then led us inside without waiting for the door to open. It was a sprawling, one-story house with red tile floors and dark wooden ceilings, built after the war as Los Alamos tried to transform itself from a bivouac into a permanent, comfortable town. Nothing was packed. There were stacks of empty boxes in the living room and the kitchen. Books overspilled the shelves, which lined every wall; half-empty coffee cups stagnated on wobbly side tables; faded Indian rugs were scattered haphazardly about the floor. I ran my fingertip along a window sill and lifted it to study the coat of dust it had collected. Soft, odorless, gray.

"Nine o'clock already?" came Adam's muffled voice from the back of the house. A moment later he appeared in the kitchen. "Couldn't have made it ten?" A dollop of toothpaste foam was escaping the left corner of his mouth. He was a tall man with a slight shuffle to his step who wore stained, too-short ties and always had dull pencils sticking out of every available pocket—pants, shirt, jacket, even the pockets of his bathrobe.

"Looks like you could use a hand with the packing," my mother said, her voice tight. She never would have dared to come right out and say that he'd promised to be ready, that she considered this to be an abuse of our goodwill.

"Since I'm being forcibly evicted, it seems fair," Adam said. Adam had lived in that house for thirty-five years, but without his wife, Angeline, who had died of ovarian cancer two years earlier, something finally had to be done. My father didn't want him living on his own, with the slick tile underfoot and neighbors whose attention was too firmly on the microscopic to notice if anything happened to the old man next door. The two of them had struck a deal: Adam could keep his driver's license if he'd move to a smaller, safer place. He was furious, but he knew he'd never pass the test if he had to take it again, so there we were, packing.

As soon as we'd finished eating the bagels we'd picked up on the way over, Adam Brooks took me aside. My parents stayed in the kitchen, as though tethered by a short leash to the gurgling coffee pot. We stood in a corner of the chaotic living room. The smell of burned crumbs from the toaster lingered in the air. Katie, seeing that I was being singled out, immediately came over and stood nearby, ready to wedge her skinny frame into our huddle. She never could bear to be shown up; any time someone demonstrated a skill, she rushed to display her own abilities, and the appearance of some new toy or piece of clothing at school would send her scurrying for her own possessions to show off.

Katie was much better suited to the sorts of projects Adam Brooks dreamed up than I was. It wasn't just her extra two and a half years that gave her such skill and confidence in matters of adventure; she had always been that way, from the moment she'd charged out of the womb feet first before the doctor could set up for the Caesarian he wanted to perform.

"Dr. Brooks," Adam said in his booming voice, though I would become the only member of the family who never got an advanced degree. I was nervous, already wary of Adam's brand of fun, so when Katie appeared, ponytail swinging, I turned my shoulder to include her. "I've got a job for you," Adam said. He had a kind look on his face, as though he were about to give me an extravagant gift, but I knew the kinds of gifts he chose: lab goggles and textbooks, little vials and jars full of rare elements, ingredients for fireworks, of no use to me.

"What job?" I asked, keeping my eyes on his tufted white hair. Perhaps, I thought hopefully, he had finally caught on to the kinds of things I was good at: sorting, alphabetizing, finding the most efficient way to fit things together.

"I need you to dig up some buried treasure," he said. His breath smelled of coffee. I wasn't sure how to take this. It could've been a joke, or some term of the secret and serious world he, my parents, and increasingly, Katie, inhabited. Not knowing what to say, I kept quiet.

"Treasure?" Katie said. "What kind of treasure?"

"I buried two big Mason jars of silver under the house when your father was a little boy. For emergencies."

"You mean like if the world blew up?" Katie asked.

"Something like that," Adam said. And I, having been raised in a house where emergencies were constantly forecast, didn't think to ask any further questions.

Most people aren't worried about the end of the world. They have a general sense of security, the tendency to postpone things, the ability to go to bed angry, a set of long-term plans. Then there are the crazies, the conspiracy theorists, the UFO watchers and Elvis worshippers who are sure the world is about to end. They stand on street corners with signs, run websites tracking the evidence, and generally set themselves apart. Most people are aware of this dichotomy.

What they don't generally experience is the third group, whose fears are fully founded and based on the probability of an astronomical event, such as the sudden extinction of the sun or the collision of a massive interstellar object with the Earth, or an understanding of the massive power in the world's nuclear arsenals. There are countless ways in which we could all be obliterated: A small but fanatical group could start a nuclear war. An accident in a lab or at one of the test sites could blow up a good chunk of the United States. A misinterpreted gesture could send a skittish Eastern country running for its red button, and we, if we survived, would be left in a barren nuclear winter. Most people are completely unaware of the incredibly close calls we have survived since man first began to play with fire, and that is how it must be; it is not practical to be conscious of our own fragility.

So when Adam said the word "emergency," we took him seriously.

"Now," he said, "there are two big jars down there full of silver in scrap and coin. Worth a lot of money. I was saving it in case the currency collapsed."

"How long have they been there?" asked Katie, her eyes growing wide.

"Let's see. It's what, 1987 now? I buried them in 1960."

"Twenty-seven years," I said. I had been drilled on math facts until I could barely blink, and by considering the numbers through the words that indicated them, I had managed.

"Good man," Adam Brooks said. "I'll give you a map, and there's a trowel and a couple of flashlights out in the lab." The lab was the garage. I stood still on my spot. It would be dark and dirty under the house. I'd seen all sorts of things crawling in the yard, snakes and spiders, and once, a scorpion.

"Can I go too?" Katie asked. "If there's two jars, we can each get one."

"You'd better ask your brother," Adam Brooks said, straightening. "He's in charge of treasure retrieval." I had thought at the time that it was because I was a boy that the task had been assigned to me, but I wonder now if it was because I was the child he considered more in need of toughening up.

"You can come," I said quickly. I would've liked to say that she could go in my place, that I would stay inside and pack books into neatly labeled boxes, but I couldn't say that to Adam Brooks as he towered over us.

"I'll get the map," he said, and disappeared into his study. Our parents were still in the kitchen, silently sipping the cooling dregs of their coffee. When Adam Brooks had a plan, they never interfered.

I tried not to look at Katie—I had no wish to see the challenge I knew would be in her freckled face—so instead I looked at the stack of papers that was nearest to me, on the scarred teak coffee table.

MEMO: PROJECT LEADERSHIP, GROUP D-55. CONFIDENTIAL.

I knew I should look away and forget it was there, but of course, I couldn't. It explained that there was a new procedure regarding the archiving of confidential files. Anything pertaining to design should be stored in locked cabinet A; testing, cabinet B; military use, cabinet C. No documents should be left on your desk when you leave the room. Should you observe—

Suddenly I was being choked by my collar. Someone was yelling, but in my struggle to breathe, I couldn't understand. I could smell the cedar of his aftershave, the sensation oddly heightened in my state of oxygen deprivation. Intrigued and startled, I did not struggle.

"Put him down!" Katie shrieked, as though she, at eighty-two pounds, could have done anything about it if he had refused. She was trembling; she had put herself in danger by confronting him. Once my feet hit the ground, I began to make out Adam's words.

"You know better than this! This is a question of national security! Do you want the FBI knocking on your door? Do you?" At the time I believed him—I had done something terrible. But now I wonder: at sixty-eight, was he still at the cutting edge of the research? He knew secrets, certainly, but this memo was about file cabinets. If it was private, he never should've brought it home and left it out. I find it more likely now that it was just a security reflex from the days when his work really was secret and dangerous. But that didn't stop him from unleashing his wrath on the eight-year-old Ben Brooks, that disappointing child who sat in his bedroom scribbling pages in a notebook while his sister set off impressive explosions in the back yard. My breath was still coming in gasps, my throat burning.

"I didn't know it was a secret," I said. "I'm sorry. I won't do it again." A faint thrill of hope struck me; perhaps, as a punishment, I would be deprived of the fun of the treasure hunt. But Adam let it drop. He handed me a folded, yellowed piece of paper that looked in danger of falling apart. Then he turned his back and resumed his place in the kitchen; we were on our own.

Katie looked over my shoulder as I gingerly unfolded the map. I could smell her bubblegum and feel her cool breath on my ear. The map displayed an irregular polygon, a rectangle with a trapezoid stuck on the end. I turned it around and around and finally figured out which room was which. There were two small x's, each with lines showing the distance from the walls. I knew where the opening to the crawlspace was on the side of the house, covered by a wire mesh panel to keep animals out, but beyond that, I had no idea how I was going to translate this map into the dusty, dark reality under the house.

I briefly considered an appeal to my mother, who, with her soft turtlenecks and pale lipstick, was slightly more likely than the other adults to offer comfort, but she was already irritated by the state of the house, and I knew better than to make requests of her when she wasn't in the mood. If I had asked for a different job instead, my father and Adam would've laughed and pounded me on the back and told me to get down there. It wasn't malice, but a misconception so deep that its possessors didn't even recognize it.

"Come on." Katie dragged me by the hand to the lab. We found a pair of trowels and two red plastic flashlights and carried our tools out into the yard.

I stood in the New Mexico sunshine for perhaps thirty seconds, listening for voices from the house, hoping that someone would come out to tell us never mind, they'd forgotten that the silver had already been retrieved, or that it wasn't worth much after all and we'd be put to better use indoors. But no one came.

"Come on!" Katie was getting impatient, as though we were waiting in line for a carnival ride rather than preparing to carry out an assigned chore.

"You can go alone," I said. "If you're so excited." I reached down to swat away the invisible bug that I was sure was climbing on my leg. "I could time you."

"No way, chicken!" She tugged on her ponytail to tighten its band. She had me cornered and she knew it. This was payback for all those times when she'd wanted my help with some project or experiment, and I'd elected to read, or practice the piano, or run as fast as I could up and down the block with my stopwatch trying to beat my previous record. If I didn't go down there, neither would she, and I'd be held responsible. I didn't know what Adam would do if we came back without the jars, but I didn't want to find out.

She stood behind me while I prepared to pry the cover off the crawlspace. I smelled mildew. The cover was more secure than it looked, and I tried to wedge it off with the tip of my trowel, but it didn't budge. I looked back at Katie for support, but she just cracked her gum and put one hand on her hip.

I strained and tugged and all of a sudden, I was flying through the air with the cover in my hands. I landed on my rear end a few feet back. Katie laughed. She would've done it easily. Gracefully.

Embarrassed but not injured, I handed her the map, took a flashlight, and prepared to go in. There was less than two feet between the ground and the house, and I could already feel the grime settling in my pores. I tried to imagine Adam Brooks climbing down here to place the jars to begin with, but I couldn't picture him as anything other than a stiff, slightly deaf old man.

I took a deep breath of above-ground air and aimed myself head-first into the void. The first thing I noticed was the cold. Beyond the small window provided by the opening to the outside, the darkness was near complete. Once I got myself all the way inside and aimed the flashlight, I could see only about three feet in front of me. There was something sharp digging into my left forearm. There were pipes overhead, and the ground was littered with the carcasses of vines that had tried to grow their way in from outside and withered in the absence of light and moisture.

For a moment, I feared that Katie would not come. She had no obligation here, and I wasn't at all sure that I could locate the jars myself. If I'd been nearly strangled just for reading a paper that was face-up in the living room, what kind of punishment would this failure bring? There was no precedent among the Brookses for backing out of things.

Mercifully, Katie's freckled face soon appeared in the hole and she shimmied in on her elbows. "All right," she said. "Let's do this thing." Her gum was gone; she must have swallowed it. I felt, for a moment, that I was going to be sick, and I concentrated on keeping my breakfast where it belonged. My throat stung with acid.

"We'll each take one jar," Katie said, spreading the map between us. "Divide and conquer. Which one do you want?"

"Can't we do it together?" I said. "One jar at a time?"

"No," she said, "faster this way. I'll take the far one—" she pointed to one of the x's— "and you can take this one. We'll just get as close as we can to where it looks like it is, and dig. They can't be buried very deep. And if we don't find anything after a few inches, we try again in a new spot."

"I don't know," I said, as though we had an alternative. "That sounds like a lot of digging. And if we don't find them—"

"We'll find them," she said. She studied the map intently for half a minute more, then lifted her head. "Okie dokie. See you in a few." And she crawled off toward the other end of the house. I shone my flashlight on her as she went, watching her snake-like progress, choking on the dust she kicked up as she disappeared behind a cement pillar. Then the noise of her crawling stopped and she began to dig. I studied the dirt in which I was lying. It was pale, more like sand than soil. There were all sorts of things in it, bits of dried leaves, pebbles, dead bugs. Poor bugs. Thousands of bugs, sow bugs, cockroaches, ants, spiders, must have died here this year alone, and in the space of the universe, as Adam Brooks had told us again and again, I was really no greater than they were. I thought of our parents in the bright kitchen, the tubs of cream cheese still on the table. That was where I wanted to be. But Adam Brooks was there. No matter how much I hated this dusty, buggy crawlspace, it was better than facing him.

I crawled to the side wall where the map indicated my jar would be and began scooting forward, trying to match the distance proportionally with the diagram. It was hard to gauge distance in the dark. I chose a place that seemed about right, rested the flashlight on the ground beside me, and began jabbing the pointy tip of the trowel into the dirt. The dust got in my eyes and throat. I wished I'd thought to bring water. I heard footsteps, clomping with a slight shuffle: Adam Brooks was moving around overhead. I began to dig faster. I could hear Katie digging in some distant corner. The ground was harder than I'd imagined. Eventually, I managed to dig four or five inches in and found nothing. My hands were chafing from squeezing the trowel. I moved over a few feet and started digging again.

I was on my fourth hole when I heard Katie shriek. "Got it!" she said. I was relieved—at least we wouldn't have to return to Adam Brooks with nothing—but I was also disappointed. Though I'd been telling myself again and again that I was glad she was there, I knew then that I had wanted to find the jars myself.

"Great," I called. "We can find the other one faster if we're both looking for it, and then we can get out of here."

"No way," she said. "That one's yours." I heard her approaching, shimmying around the poles that supported the house, pushing the jar in front of her, and then the beam of her flashlight came into view. I kept digging and concentrated on not crying. If there was anything worse than failing to do what Adam Brooks had asked of you, it was crying in front of him. Last time I'd done it, when I'd slammed my finger in the front door, he'd given me a furious lecture about pain and how I didn't know the meaning of the word. My mother had waited until he was finished before quietly offering an ice pack.

Katie watched me dig. I switched the trowel from my left hand to my right, then back again. She tilted her jar, and we both listened to the clink of the silver inside. Finally, she took pity on me. She looked at the map, then shone her flashlight up and down the space in which I was working, and selected a spot of her own. We worked a long time in silence, side by side.

I had no way of telling time, but I could count the holes: thirty-one. Thirty-one holes, and no second jar. My hands were blistered. My knees ached. The cold had not softened, even as the sun had presumably risen higher in the sky. I felt as though the floors were pressing down on us from above, sinking with the weight of every parental footstep. I rested my cheek for a moment on my hand, then lifted my head.

"It's not here," I said. I hadn't planned to say it. I wished I could take it back.

"Of course it's here," Katie said. "It's on the map."

"This is where it's supposed to be. We've checked this whole part."

"We have to keep looking," she said. "We can't go back up there without it. He'll kill us."

"He won't kill *you*," I said. I pictured his face, the vein in his neck bulging, his cheeks red with rage.

"Do you really think we can go up without it?" Katie asked. I couldn't tell if the edge in her voice was concern or hope. Her hands, like mine, were stiff and raw, and she was shivering. Could it be that she, too, had had enough? That what she needed was a hero, someone to lead her to the exit?

"It's freezing," I said, gathering steam. "And this map is no good." I started crawling toward the door. Adam or no Adam, we weren't doing anyone any good down there. After a moment, Katie followed.

The sun was so bright that we both stood blinking for a full minute before we could get our bearings. My mind swam with the process of digging, as waves still roll beneath you when you come ashore after hours of swimming in the ocean. I wanted to stay forever in the sun, out of the spooky darkness but not yet facing the judgment that we both knew would fall on us.

"We'd better go in," Katie said. My terror grew deeper. My whole body began to tremble, not enough to see, but enough to render me unsteady. Katie stood tall and sturdy. She spoke their language. She could be my interpreter.

We brushed the dirt from our clothes, and I waited for my big sister to lead me gently inside, to take charge, to explain what had happened and how hard we'd tried, how even she, older and wiser, had been unable to find the second jar, but she did not. Stubborn Katie, already digging her heels in for what would be a lifelong battle over credit for her work.

It was either go inside to announce surrender or slink back into the dusty darkness, but I couldn't see how we'd find the jar even if we went back. My mind was set: I led the way into the kitchen where the three adults were gathered. Our parents stood at the counter packing boxes with Adam Brooks behind them, supervising. Katie followed me, cradling her prize. I wanted to turn and run, but I knew I couldn't escape. Katie nudged me in the back with her elbow. I had started this capitulation; it was mine to carry through.

"She found one of them," I said, aiming the announcement nowhere in particular. I tried to take a deep breath but it caught halfway through. I had to say it. "I couldn't find mine." From behind, Katie plucked a withered vine from my hair.

"What do you mean, you couldn't find it?" Adam Brooks said in the famous exasperated tone he used to take with colleagues who didn't immediately grasp the complex physics of a solution he'd proposed. "I gave you the map."

"We were looking that whole time," I said.

"That jar is worth a lot of money," Adam Brooks said, stretching his arms out to Katie and taking her jar, wiping the last of its dust on his pants. "It's not something you can just quit on because you're tired."

"We tried," Katie said, her voice now no more than a squeak. Her lower lip began to tremble. Our parents stood quietly at the kitchen counter, wrapping plates in old newspapers.

"Tried?" Adam said. "How hard can it be?" He was speaking only to me now. "Just follow the map. Your sister managed it." And I wanted to say, Katie couldn't find this jar either. I wanted to say, you're the one who drew the map to begin with. You hid them too well. It's your fault, not mine. And perhaps he knew that, and was angry mostly at himself, but I couldn't understand that. I was only eight.

"There was no way to measure," I said. "We dug a zillion holes." That was all I had in me, and a glance at his tensed jaw told me I'd said too much already. I took two stumbling steps backward. I saw my father look up for a moment, as though he were going to come to my defense, but Adam had taken charge. He would issue the punishment, banning me from the dinner table that night and the next and confiscating two months' allowance as a down payment on what I owed him, and no one would dare to object. I was right and he would win anyway. Adam Brooks raved on about what a simple task it was, how incompetent I must be. My parents kept their eyes on their packing. Katie opened her mouth to speak, then closed it again.

And still, thirty years later, she won't stand up for me. She won't tell Carl Chesterfeld that I am her brother, that I belong here. How can I be sure that I won't unwittingly act just the same if I have a family of my own? I picked up other patterns from them. Robin is often baffled by the things I find myself expecting: detailed explanations of the process by which minor decisions were reached, the exact source of every quotation used in conversation, the precise name for every food we eat. I know where I learned to expect those things. This inheritance is, I see now, what I have been afraid of, what has bubbled up in my stomach every time Robin has raised the question of children. Here it is: the decision I have been unable to make for four years.

I sit for a while with my choice, listening to the rise and fall of voices admiring my tyrant of a grandfather. This is such a strange city, so long on intellect, so short on empathy. I miss New York.

After a while, Katie comes into my hideout and sits beside me. "It's the end of an era," she says.

"I don't know that it is," I tell her. "Can't you still hear his voice in your head?"

"I suppose so." I want to hate her, but I don't. She wasn't the one behind it all; she simply fell into line. "I don't know what it'll be like here without him," she says. "Los Alamos, I mean."

"It'll go on," I say. She shifts, uncomfortable, as though I have insulted her. "Remember that time we crawled under the house for those jars of silver?"

She looks puzzled for a moment, then smiles. "I'd forgotten." There are deep lines around her eyes and at the corners of her mouth that I didn't notice earlier.

"It's probably still there," I say. "That other jar."

"That's right," she says. "You never did find it." After all these years, this is the thing she thinks to say. Adam is gone, and nothing has changed. It is as though she has come on purpose to confirm my decision: we are irreversibly warped. Unfit to reproduce.

"Come on out," Katie says. "People are leaving. They'll want to say goodbye." There's no use in arguing. I follow her back into the hall. I feel different, now that I know that we are the end of the line; we'd better make something of ourselves, Katie and I.

I am exhausted when I get to my hotel. Robin will be upset. I imagine the sound of her voice as she takes the news, trying not to cry, because she'll know what it means: the end of us. She might try to reason with me. She might yell, or break down weeping. I'd better call her before I get worked up over a conversation that hasn't happened yet. As I wait for her to answer, I feel my deepest loss: she is about to answer the phone for the last time as my loving, hopeful partner.

"You survived," she says. "How're you feeling? In need of someone to talk to who isn't a scientist?"

I mean to ease into it, to say yes, I miss you, it went fine, something strange has happened, but instead, the decision spills from me. "I can't be a father, Robin."

"Did something happen?" she asks gently. "You're upset. Let's talk about this when a little time has passed."

"Something did happen," I tell her. "Thirty years ago." I give her the nutshell version of our voyage under the house, of Adam's brutal punishment, of my family's refusal to defend me before him. "Not even a word," I say. "All three of them just stood there and let him pummel me. And that's the stock I'm from. I can't pass that on."

Robin begins to laugh. She laughs so long and hard that I'm sure tears are streaming down her cheeks and she's clutching her stomach. I hold the hotel phone away from my ear for a minute and when I bring it back, she's still laughing. Finally, she pauses.

"What's so goddamn funny?" I ask.

"That's your reason? That's why you've been so afraid all this time?"

"You find that amusing?" I ask. I can't help it: I start to cry.

"Don't you get it, Ben?" she says. "You're nothing like them. I don't know how a family like that produced someone as stable as you." Another giggle escapes her. "That's the whole point. You *can't* do what they do. That's why they hurt you so much. That's why you ended up here, with me."

I consider this. She could be right.

"Now get back here and make love to me," she says. "We've got a lot of planning to do. We have to pick names and paint the nursery," she says.

"Come back to me," she says. "Come back."

ACKNOWLEDGMENTS

I COULD NOT HAVE written this book without the unyielding support of my family. Thank you to my parents, Lisa and Dave, my sister and brother-in-law, Elizabeth and Max, and my grandparents, Boz, Malcolm, Mary, and Bob. I also owe an eternal debt to Matthew Fickett, whose stories inspired me and whose friendship sustains me.

ABOUT THE AUTHOR

AMY KNIGHT IS A civil rights and criminal defense attorney. She lives in Tucson, Arizona with her dogs, Oscar and Ruby.

author photo by Richard Whitmer

CPSIA information can be obtained
at www.ICGtesting.com
Printed in the USA
LVOW11s1934011217
558236LV00002B/9/P